Val longs to feel loved and accepted, but at what cost . . . ?

"Val, you're in denial," Joel groaned in exasperation, clenching his teeth. "Can't you see that the Family has psychologically manipulated you? They'll use you to peddle Father Elijah's writings and build his empire.

"You're not working for God, Val. *This* stuff isn't the gospel of Christ!" he spat angrily, pointing to her stack of literature. As soon as the words were out of his mouth, he wanted to snatch them back. *Nice going, Bennigan. Drive her away with another temper tantrum.*

"Val, I'm sorry, . . ." Joel began. More frustrated than he could ever recall being in his life, he drove his fingers through his hair and struggled to regain control.

But Val had seen the anger flash in his eyes—then the coldness, as if the blue orbs had been chipped from a glacier. . . . "Denial?" she echoed. "I'm not denying anything! You're denying the CLDL's true devotion to God's work!"

ELIZABETH MURPHY, author of *Not for a Million Dollars* and *Dealing with Destructive Cults,* borrows from her own past experiences as a member of a religious cult for this, her first published novel.

A prolific writer, Elizabeth is also wife to Roy and Mom to three strapping sons. She resides with her family in Columbia, Maryland.

Love's
Tender Gift

Elizabeth Murphy

Heartsong Presents

To Roy,
my very own Prince Charming.

A note from the Author:
*I love to hear from my readers! You may write to me at
the following address:* **Elizabeth Murphy**
Author Relations
P.O. Box 719
Uhrichsville, OH 44683

ISBN 1-55748-701-4

LOVE'S TENDER GIFT

Cover illustration by Brian Bowman.

PRINTED IN THE U.S.A.

one

"I won't leave you—and that's final!"

Val Packard stood, hands on hips, glaring down at her roommate with the sternest, most authoritative posture her slight frame could muster.

"Just look at yourself," Val said. "You're as pale as a ghost—no, amend that, you're practically green around the gills. I'm staying home. The Bible study can wait until next week."

Tess McGowen peered up from beneath Val's tartan blanket, her feverish body huddled into a pathetic ball on their couch.

"Honest, Val, I'm OK," she wheezed. "It's just a touch of beginning-of-semester flu. It's a requirement for history majors in the graduate program, y'know."

"Oh, *please!*" groaned Val.

"Really, you've gotten me a blanket and a cup of flu therapy—you can't do anything more right now," Tess insisted, waving Val toward the front door of their tiny apartment. "I'll be fine, but you need to escape my germs—and make some new friends, preferably some healthy ones," she quipped.

"Yeah, you've got a point," Val conceded, her heart still heavy with misgivings. "But I still don't feel right leaving you."

"I promise—cross my heart—that if I get worse,

I'll call the church on this piece of marvelous modern technology," said Tess, waving the telephone receiver.

"OK, OK, I'm going." Val pulled on her burgundy down jacket. "I know when I'm not wanted," she sniffed, stopping in front of the hall mirror to push her long auburn hair up under her woolen cap. Her face showed a vulnerability she tried hard to hide, and at the moment her jade green eyes betrayed worry.

"Seriously, Tess, I'm not looking forward to walking into a roomful of strangers by myself. I don't know anyone at Faith Bible. It's different for you. You grew up with these folks."

"And that's why I know they'll welcome you," sputtered Tess between coughs. She reached for her hot drink. "I've already warned them about my new roommate. . . that you're from Maryland and you're taking a master's degree in journalism at Kent State University and, as far as I know, you're not an ax murderer. So just ask for the assistant pastor, Joel Bennigan. He's leading the Young Singles' Bible Study tonight." Tess sighed as she collapsed back onto her mound of cushions.

Still not entirely convinced, Val reached for her knapsack hanging on the back of the kitchen door. Half-heartedly, she stuffed in her Bible and notepad, then frowned as she eyed her sick friend.

Tess waved her away. "I promise I'll call. How can I get any rest with you hovering over me? Get thee to a nunnery—or at least to the Bible study."

Val couldn't help cracking a smile. She'd known Tess less than a week and already she'd grown to appreciate her roommate's dry sense of humor. The student housing office at the university had certainly made a good match this time.

"You've made your point," Val said. "I guess being a graduate student doesn't give a person immunity from viruses. I'll see you later."

She pulled her jacket tighter around her slim body and ducked her head against a cold wind that gusted up Main Street. The damp night air slid its chilly fingers down her neck, and she huddled into her up-turned collar. She wished her car wasn't on the blink again. *That car spends more time in the shop than on the road,* she sighed.

The street lamps reflected brightly off the wet black street, giving the impression of early Christmas lights. But Val wasn't filled with any spirit of warmth or expectancy. She was new in this town—new and alone—except for Tess. *But that's how it's always been,* she thought.

In the distance, an evening train moaned mournfully into the black night as it began its lonely trek across Ohio. She shivered, more from the loneliness in her heart than the cold numbing her limbs.

Main Street wound its way up a hill for at least a mile, and Val made the climb at a brisk pace. At the top stood Faith Bible, a huge, light brick church dating back to the 1950's. The yellow glow from its windows offered a welcome that made her eyes mist with unaccustomed tears.

Slipping inside the building, Val pulled off her cap and mittens and stamped her feet to get the circulation going before hurrying down the long corridors, following the pen and ink signs for the Bible study.

Peering through the glass door panels as she hurried by, she spied a gathering of Sunday school teachers, a budget meeting, and a seniors' social. By all accounts, Faith Bible was a vibrant, thriving community, and Val felt glad she'd joined this church family.

Finally, just as she was beginning to wonder just how big one sprawling church building could be, the paper trail reached its destination. The sign on the door cheerfully announced: "Yes! You've found the right place—the Young Singles' Bible Study! No need to knock, just c'mon in!" Val smiled. *The singles sounded like a friendly bunch, all right.*

Just then, she caught a glimpse of another sign on the opposite door. "Adult Children of Alcoholics" it announced in stenciled red letters. Val's heart skipped a beat. This was the last thing she wanted to see, but the sign seemed to beckon her. Her legs felt as heavy as tree stumps. She couldn't, wouldn't move towards that door.

Get hold of yourself, girl, she chided. *You don't need them. Those groups are for losers. OK, OK, your childhood might not have been great . . . but you don't need that. You're making it just fine by yourself. And that's the way it's going to stay.*

She took three deep breaths. Then three more. But her heart wouldn't quiet down. Unbidden and unwanted, old, long-suppressed memories forced themselves into her consciousness.

A little girl, eight years old. Long auburn hair hanging uncombed; her dress, soiled. She'd fallen down and grazed her elbow badly on the concrete. Holding her bleeding arm, Val ran home, weeping and calling for her mother. As she dashed into the dark house and through the messy kitchen, she slipped on spilled milk.

"Mommy! Mommy! Where are you?" she cried, her distress mounting.

Her wails echoed through the silent house. Choking back sobs and wrapping a dish towel around her aching elbow, she picked her way from room to room, peering inside each.

"Mommy! I need you!"

Panic clutched her. It started in her throat and spread throughout her chest. A familiar, sick feeling formed in the pit of her stomach. Her mouth tasted stale and sour, like the out-dated milk in the refrigerator. Slowly, she climbed the stairs. The door at the top was closed. Her mother's bedroom. Usually, she didn't dare go in there.

"Mommy . . ."

Instinctively, she lowered her voice as she pushed open the heavy wooden door. Odors of stale whiskey and cigarette smoke assaulted her senses. The TV blared so loudly that her ears hurt. It took several seconds for her eyes to adjust to the darkness.

Then Val saw her mother, face down across the bed, her head dangling over the edge. A glass tumbler had fallen from her limp hand, its sticky, smelly contents oozing into the stained carpet.

"Mommy?"

Hesitantly, Val touched her mother's shoulder. The woman stirred. "Leave me alone!" she snapped, her words slurred.

"Mommy, I hurt my arm. . . ." Val whimpered.

"Get out!" Mrs. Packard shot back. "Don't you dare come into my room again!"

Val saw a monster—long dark hair dirty and matted, eyes bloodshot, skin pale with a gray cast. Frightened, the little girl backed out and closed the door. Ever since her father had died in Vietnam that year, she had often seen her mother like this.

She fled to her room and flung herself on the narrow bed. Her elbow throbbed painfully, but her heart hurt worse, much worse.

"Maybe if I'd been a better girl, Daddy wouldn't have died and Mommy wouldn't be like this," Val sobbed into her pillow. "Maybe if I were a better girl, Mommy would love me . . . ."

"Hey, pretty lady, can I interest you in a good Bible study?" A deep male voice interrupted her thoughts.

Val swung around and stared up into a handsome face with the craggy look of an unfinished sculpture. The man's angular profile struck her as compelling, and his tawny-gold hair gave him an almost leonine appearance. He towered over her, his broad shoulders nearly filling the doorway. She caught a dizzying whiff of his musky aftershave.

Great! From nightmare to dreamboat in a matter of seconds, Val mused, enjoying this pleasant distraction from her ugly memories and roller-coaster emotions. Suddenly, she found herself chuckling in relief.

"And the lady has a sense of humor." The stranger smiled and extended a large, square hand, his intense blue eyes twinkling with both vivaciousness and kindness. "Hello, I'm Joel Bennigan. Welcome to the Young Singles' Bible Study."

"Oh. . .so *you're* Joel Bennigan," Val echoed, feeling a warm sense of pleasure at his masculine attention.

"Yeah, last time I checked." He ran a hand through the thick waves of his hair.

"My roommate told me to ask for you," Val said.

"Oh. . .so *you're* Tess' roomie," Joel exclaimed, reaching out to engulf both her hands in his. "Hear you've got a pretty good bedside manner with our dear sick sister."

Val smiled. *I like this guy.*

He motioned her into the warm, cozy den and took her jacket. Three tweed sofas clustered around the roaring fire practically filled the room. A circle of friendly faces looked up from their Bibles. "Hi!" chorused the singles of Faith Bible.

"Friends, may I present Miss Val Packard," Joel announced with a flourish. "Tess' roommate."

Suddenly Val found herself surrounded by half a dozen people, shaking her hand, welcoming her, shepherding her over to a couch.

"I'm Flo," chirped a small blond woman. "And this is Cathy. We're in several of Tess' classes. She told us you'd be coming."

"Hi, Val," someone else said. "Welcome!"

Amid the happy banter, Val could concentrate on only one person—Joel Bennigan. He stood by the fireplace, arms folded over his chest. His straight nose and clearly defined chin gave him a patrician air. She could feel his blue eyes on her, and a blush rose involuntarily to her cheeks.

"How about some hot chocolate, Val?" he offered. "Our Ohio weather gets nippy this time of year. It'll help chase the chill."

"Yes, thank you, I'd like that."

Joel's well-muscled body moved across the room with grace as he fetched the beverage. His hand brushed hers as she took the steaming mug, and his gaze lingered a fraction of a second longer than necessary for polite social interaction, it seemed.

Shyly, Val turned away and sat down as far from Joel Bennigan as she could manage, busying herself with unpacking her Bible, pad, and pencils from her knapsack.

While she was thus occupied, Joel stepped into his leadership role. Picking up his Bible from the end table, he began, his rich baritone voice growing serious. "Let's continue our study of grace. Our brother Paul was a wounded man, as we all are. In his zeal to win God's approval, he kept the Jewish law compulsively. Haven't we all tried to be 'good enough' for God?" He paused, his eyes scanning the room. "Let's admit it. I know I have.

"But through Jesus, Paul learned the most important lesson of his life—that what the law could not do, grace has already done," Joel continued, his eyes burning with an inner fire. "Through Christ, Paul was justified. Through Christ, Paul was loved. While still in his sin, through Christ, Paul was accepted. And that, my brothers and sisters, is grace.

"Listen to the joy—and relief—in Paul's cry: 'And the life which I now live in the flesh I live by faith in the Son of God, who loved me and gave Himself for me' (Gal. 2:20). Paul didn't have to earn God's love. And because Christ loved Paul, *Paul* could love Paul. Through grace, he found that he belonged. Through grace, Paul came home."

Val sat spellbound. The man spoke with such power, she thought. Standing by the fireplace, one arm casually flung over the mantel, the other holding a well-worn leather Bible, Joel Bennigan exuded confidence. Even in casual tan Dockers and a red plaid shirt open at the neck, he had an unmistakable air of authority. And his penetrating eyes held the color of the sky on a clear summer afternoon.

Suddenly, that blue gaze was resting on her, with the effect of a bolt of lightning setting a tree afire. A shiver—of delight, of fear, of apprehension—she couldn't tell which—tingled up Val's spine. She couldn't look away. She felt drawn into the fire burning in his eyes.

"Through Christ's healing love, we can all come home," Joel said slowly, reverently, his gaze never leaving her flushed face. "Thanks to grace, we can all say with Paul that He 'loved me and gave Himself for me.'"

Slowly, Joel's words penetrated Val's consciousness—*love, grace, home*. She felt acutely embarrassed, as if his message were for her, and her alone. Surely everyone else in the room knew it was for Val Packard, the girl without a home.

Did she really believe in God's grace, she wondered, or did she still have to prove herself worthy of love, over and over again?

Loud, frantic knocking at the door startled her and caused her to jump.

A short, middle-aged man tumbled in, almost out of breath. "Reverend Joel, thank God you're still here!" he huffed. "It's my son—you've got to talk to him!"

Joel calmly put his hand on the distraught man's shoulder. "What is it, Dan?"

"Kevin's just come home. . .from the cult! But something's wrong. Something's *very* wrong!"

two

"I think Kevin's been brainwashed!" cried Dan Milford.

Val's heart went out to the man, and she watched Joel carefully, eager to see what he would do next.

"I know, Dan. It's mind control," Joel said, his voice gentle with compassion.

"But what can we do? His mother and I asked Kevin to come home for a few days to talk about his new commitment to the Children of Last Days Light. But he's not making any sense!"

Joel slung his arm easily around Mr. Milford's shoulder and started toward the door. "We'll talk to Kevin," he said. "All night if we have to. You go on home, Dan, and keep an eye on him. I'll pick up some books at my office and come right over."

Dan Milford nodded, his hunched shoulders relaxing visibly. "Mary and I are out of our depth, Reverend Joel," he confessed. "We don't know enough about cults to reason with our son. We—we're stymied. . . ."

"Don't worry. With the Lord's help, we'll reach him," Joel said. Then, turning to the study group, he announced, "Sorry to break up the party early, folks. Please pray for us."

❧

As Val stepped out of Faith Bible Church, a warm

glow flickered through her in spite of the biting wind howling around the parking lot. *Joel Bennigan does more than just preach the love of God,* she thought. *He lives it.* Somehow, she knew the Milford family was in good hands.

Yes, there was something special about Joel Bennigan. A spark of life. A living flame. She wanted to witness it again, maybe to draw near enough to warm herself. . .to come in from the cold.

The wind tossed the last few leaves of autumn across the gravel parking lot. Val shivered as it whipped around her slender, jeans-clad legs. She'd just reached the corner of Main and Lincoln when a red Blazer 4 X 4 pulled up beside her.

"Hey, pretty lady, need a lift?" Joel Bennigan's grinning face appeared in the rolled-down window, his even white teeth gleaming in the light from the street lamp.

"Well, n—not really. . ." she stammered. "But it is kind of cold out here."

"OK, then, hop in."

Easier said than done. Val needed a hand to navigate the high step up to the four-wheel-drive vehicle. Again, the electricity of Joel's touch startled her. Trying to ignore her racing pulse, she concentrated on giving directions to her apartment.

"It's a long walk on a cold night," Joel noted.

"Don't I know? But my clunker's in the shop again. You know the type—spends more time in the shop than on the road," Val explained, trying to quell her nervousness with chatter.

"Ha! Yes, I know the type well. So do many folks in our church. You'll have to get acquainted with Faith Bible's Car Ministry."

"Car Ministry?"

"Yep. It's a Christian ministry for the twentieth century. Several shade-tree mechanics from church volunteer their skills. In return, the unmechanical owner volunteers time for some worthy cause."

"I like that," Val mused. "And, boy, could I use some help with my car."

"Yeah—you and a lot of others. Especially around here. The economy's been terrible for ages. Not much public transportation, either—except campus buses, of course. But many seniors and students and single moms need help keeping their cars running—and you know what the Epistle of James says. . ."

"Refresh my memory."

"James—second chapter—'If a brother or sister is ill-clad and in lack of daily food and one of you says to them, "Go in peace, be warmed and filled," without giving them the things needed for the body, what does it profit? So faith by itself, if it has no works, is dead.'

"Or, let's update that thought," Joel continued. "If a brother or sister has brake trouble and you say, 'See you later,' what kind of Christian love is that?"

Val chuckled at Joel's modernized interpretation, falling easily into the routine: "I get the point. 'As ye would that men should tune up your engine, do ye even so to them?' How can I get involved?"

"Well, dear sister, that just happens to be one of my

ministries," said Joel as he flashed a grin. "We use my folks' garage—they've got a huge spread outside town. Maybe the boys and I can take a look next time your car acts up."

"I'd appreciate that," said Val gratefully.

They rode for a few minutes in silence. Val twisted at her purse strap, casting about for something to say. She threw a sidelong glance at Joel. His serene face betrayed none of the nervousness she felt. "So you're on your way to talk to Kevin Milford?" she asked as he slowed down for a red light.

"Yes. Kevin Milford is Mary and Dan's only child. They were crushed when he joined the Children of Last Days Light."

"The religious cult?"

"Yes." Joel's classically handsome features altered with his frown as he skillfully negotiated a tricky turn. "The CLDL—as they're known around here—hides behind the Bible. They say they're Christians, but when you examine their teachings—as the Lord instructed us to do—well, it's plain they're anything but followers of Christ. They're driven by hatred and fear. They do enormous damage to their members— emotionally, spiritually, and even physically."

"Has Kevin been living with them long?"

"No, thank God. Only a few days. But they worked on him for months to persuade him to move into their commune on Oak Street."

Following Val's directions, Joel turned into the driveway of a wooden frame Victorian house divided into three student apartments. He killed the motor.

"Kevin's a freshman at KSU," Joel added, turning toward Val. An incredible sadness filled his eyes. "Cults often pick on freshmen—kids away from home for the first time. I see it all the time. It's almost criminal." He shook his head.

"I'd like to learn more," Val volunteered. "I find it appalling that they get away with this."

"I'd be glad to help in any way I can," Joel answered. An easy smile played at the corners of his mouth as his eyes rested on her face. "Let's get together and I'll pass along some information on the cult and also get you involved with our Car Ministry. Here's my card," he said, opening his wallet.

His broad face broke into a devastating grin as he pressed the card into her hand. "I'm glad you've decided to make Faith Bible your church home, Val. I'd like to chat some more, but I've got to get to the Milfords'."

She nodded and took a deep breath, wondering how one smile could thrill her so. "Thanks, Joel. I appreciate the ride home."

"My pleasure. And, Val, please pray for me that the Holy Spirit will guide me tonight. Kevin needs to see through the cult's deception and realize that only Christ can heal his brokenness."

"I'll pray for you. I promise. Good night."

Val stood in the doorway, watching Joel's Blazer pull out of her driveway.

Suddenly, he stopped and rolled down the window. "Hey—you never told me anything about yourself, mystery lady!" he shouted against the wind.

"Later!"

"You got yourself a date!" He revved the motor and disappeared down the street.

Val pulled out his card and, under the dim porch light, examined it like a treasure she'd just unearthed. "Joel Bennigan, Assistant Pastor, Faith Bible Church," it stated in bold black letters. Underneath Joel's name was a Bible verse: "For by grace you have been saved through faith" (Eph. 2:8).

"Joel Bennigan," she repeated the name several times, savoring the feel of it in her mouth. It reverberated in her head like music. The memory of his blue eyes meeting hers caused her to tremble slightly.

Don't kid yourself, she sighed. *Joel Bennigan is a handsome, charismatic man of God. He's just trying to make you feel welcome at his church. What would he want with someone like you?*

Quickly, she stuffed the card in her pocket and fled inside to the safety of her apartment.

❧

A dusky rose dawn had only begun to seep into the inky sky as Val shuffled into the kitchen and snapped on the bare overhead light. She checked the digital clock on the stove. 5:31 A.M. Her muscles ached from lack of sleep.

All night, visions of Joel Bennigan had danced in her head—Joel's pure, clear blue eyes studying her; Joel's huge hand brushing against hers; Joel's rich laughter that seemed to invite her into a whole new world. . . .

Is there no rest from this guy? Get a grip, Val. He's

way out of your league. She fired up the percolator, moving around the tiny kitchen quietly so as not to wake Tess. Her roommate had already been asleep when Val had run into the apartment last night, clutching Joel's card, his last words still ringing in her head like the refrain from a sweet romantic song: "You got yourself a date!"

Promises, promises. I'll believe it when I see it. Val sighed as she poured her mug of coffee. The brew was just the way she liked it—black, fragrant, and strong. She inhaled its pungent aroma deeply and suddenly felt better about facing the day. She pulled her Bible from its home on the hutch and plopped down at the kitchen table.

Val loved her morning ritual of rising early, brewing coffee, and spending time with God before the rest of the world started moving. It was a habit she'd acquired in her childhood—but back then, of course, she'd drunk hot chocolate, not coffee.

Hot chocolate. . . The memory of Joel Bennigan's hand grazing hers as she reached for the steaming mug re-awakened the same thrills which had coursed up and down her spine in his presence. That disturbing, powerful presence that rattled her deepest feminine self. The unsettling way his gaze lingered on her face, as if he could see into her soul. The fire that burned in those eyes as he had opened the Scriptures to the study group. . . .

Enough! Every single girl in church must have a crush on him. And he has to keep his distance. He's a minister of the gospel, after all. . . . Val wasn't comfortable with her prickly defensiveness, but she'd learned early that people couldn't be trusted, especially people who were supposed to care about you. . . .

"Valerie, of course I'll come to your school play. I'm your mother. I wouldn't miss it for the world, darling."

Joan Packard's crimson lips parted in a smile as she tied the ribbons of Val's old-fashioned bonnet under the fourth-grader's chin. The drama club had worked hard to produce "Little Women" on stage, and Val felt proud to have landed a leading role.

"I'm counting on you, Mom. All the other parents will be there. You promise?"

"Cross my heart, my darling girl. You know I wouldn't let you down."

Val sighed with relief. Her mother had been cheerful and sober for days. A good sign. She'd showered and made up her face. Another good sign. They laughed and had fun as Mrs. Packard made a few last-minute alterations to Val's costume. And Val marched off to her play with high hopes. Her mother would come through for her tonight. She'd promised. She'd sit in the front row and applaud like all the other parents.

But as the performance began, Val peered out from behind the heavy stage curtain, scanning the row of seats reserved for parents. Her heart sank, as quickly and inevitably as a stone plunges to the bottom of a lake. Her mother was not there.

That time, Joan Packard didn't emerge from her room for two days. They never talked about her missing the play or Val's receiving an award for her stellar performance. Val hid the trophy under her bed and never took part in a dramatic performance again.

Even as a grown woman, seventeen years later, Val could still taste the bitter disappointment surrounding that missed performance. And not only her disappointment that night, but all the other times. All those broken promises. By fifth grade, she'd given up begging her mother to show up for events. And little by little, she'd dropped out of activities, choosing instead to hide in her room with her books.

Val sighed and took a long drink of coffee, and tried to sweep the cobwebs of memories from her mind as she opened to the Psalms. Each day, she read three, in sequence. When she'd worked her way through all 150, she started all over again. For Val, the ancient songs of praise and thanksgiving cried out to be read in the morning; she saved the other Scriptures for the rest of the day.

"I will rejoice and be glad for your steadfast love, because you have seen my affliction." The words of the thirty-first Psalm wove a cocoon of comfort around her heart. A steadfast love—a love she could depend on. That was God's promise, clear as the black and white print before her sleep-deprived eyes.

But do I really believe that promise? Sometimes I wonder. I don't see how I'm good enough to warrant steadfast love.

Outside, a few lone birds sang their welcome to the sun as it broke, glorious and golden, over the dark skyline of Kent. Their trilling—so small, yet so insistent under the canopy of space overhead—reminded Val of the words of Jesus concerning these tiny feathered friends: "Are not two sparrows sold for a penny? And not one of them will fall to the ground without your Father's will. . . . Fear not, therefore; you are of more value than many sparrows" (Matt. 10:29-31).

"I don't know, Lord. Sometimes I don't feel like I'm worth very much, even to You. Sometimes You seem so distant. How could You possibly be interested in a dull person like me?" Val murmured as she fingered the smooth ceramic finish of her coffee mug.

Her thoughts wound back to the Bible study and the conviction she'd heard in Joel Bennigan's voice as he'd talked about Christ's love. *Well, he certainly believes in the steadfast love of God,* she mused. *He called that love grace, the gift of grace . . . .*

Val closed her eyes, placing her heavy heart before the Lord. "There's something here I'm missing, Lord," she whispered. "Something about grace I just don't get. Teach me, Lord. Teach me about this grace that Joel Bennigan believes in so passionately."

She relaxed into the familiar arms of early morning quiet, broken only by bird songs, simple praises that rivaled the beauty of Handel's *Messiah*. The white morning light flooded the kitchen with a heavenly brightness, causing the darkness to flee.

three

Thirty minutes later, Val balanced a breakfast tray loaded down with scrambled eggs, toast and jelly, orange juice, and coffee as she knocked on Tess' door.

"Come in," called a sleepy voice.

"Rise and shine and give God the glory!" sang Val as she presented the spread with a flourish. "That is, if you can get up from your deathbed."

"Val, you shouldn't have!" A smile of delight danced across Tess' tired face as she struggled to sit up.

Val arranged a pillow to support her friend's back. "I know, I know. But what ya gonna do? You need some TLC and it looks like I'm chosen provider."

"Thanks. Actually, I'm starving," Tess said as she dove into the yellow mound of eggs. "Yum, this is good. Where did you learn to cook?"

"Oh, just say I had lots of practice from a young age."

Tess shot Val a puzzled look and motioned her to sit down on the edge of her bed. "Tell me about the Bible study. I want to know everything."

"Well, let's see. . .there were about eight of us. We studied Paul's teaching on grace, drank hot chocolate, huddled beside the fire. . .and I found out about the church's Car Ministry."

"Oh, yeah—why didn't I think to tell you about that?

They'll help keep you on the road."

"I hope so. And it sounds like a good way for me to get involved with a service project." Val suddenly fell silent, her thoughts straying back to the leader of the Car Ministry.

"C'mon, more!" Tess jabbed Val's arm.

"We—ll, there *is* the matter of Joel Bennigan, the world's most handsome assistant pastor."

"Ah, ha! The real truth at last. Trust a journalism grad student to get all the facts."

Val wrinkled her nose. "Hey, no fair you siccing him on me without warning."

Tess laughed, her voice still husky with cold. "Joel may be handsome, but he doesn't capitalize on his looks—at least not anymore."

"What do you mean. . .anymore?" Val's heart skipped a beat.

"Well, it's a long story, but Reverend Bennigan wasn't always a man of God," said Tess. "In fact, at one time he was most definitely a man *without* God, and an angry young man at that."

"Your turn. Now *I* want the real truth."

"Joel comes from a wealthy old family," Tess began as she stirred sugar into her coffee. "Their roots go back to the founding of Kent. They own Bennigan's Grocery chain."

"Oh—I didn't know he was one of *those* Bennigans!"

"Yeah. Who would have thunk it?" Tess sipped her orange juice. "The Bennigans are good people. They're the type who take the gospel seriously and use their wealth as Christian stewards.

"But Joel, well, for many years, he was the black sheep. He didn't want anything to do with Christ—other than showing up in church at Christmas and Easter to please his parents. He ran with a wild crowd. His interests were girls, football, beer, and brawling—and not necessarily in that order. Quite the jock, too, believe me. He left a trail of broken hearts everywhere he went."

"I can see how," Val murmured.

Tess found a more comfortable position in the bed and continued her story. "Joel's college football career was really going places back then. He was quarterback for Kent's Golden Flashes, you know. In fact, Joel was shaping up into a top-draft pick for the pros. Then he got hurt."

"What happened?"

"The Flashes were on a winning streak. It was the final game of the season, and the score was tied. Media people from all over the state were there, watching Joel. Early in the last quarter, as Joel dropped back to pass, the defense launched an all-out blitz. He was sacked viciously, and both his knees were so badly injured that he was told he could never play again."

Val gasped.

"He required almost a year of physical therapy. The media called it the greatest tragedy a football hero could suffer," Tess continued, munching a piece of toast. "But that's not how Joel sees it. At least not now."

A knowing smile crept over her lips. "Joel likes to say that God draws straight with crooked lines. That

injury led him to Christ. It showed him how tempo-
rary and fickle the glories of this world really are.
That's when he went to seminary and became a minister."

"Wow. . .what a story," Val said softly. "No wonder Joel preaches with such conviction."

Tess nodded. "You've got that right. Joel certainly
is a man acquainted with grief and pain, but that's
how he came to trust in the love of God. That's what
makes him the compassionate pastor he is today."

"'God draws straight with crooked lines,'" Val
quoted. "It takes a lot of faith to believe a statement
like that."

"Well, God's got a habit of not giving up on us until
we get the message." Tess' gentle laugh rippled
through the air as she handed Val the breakfast tray
and scooted to the edge of the bed.

"Val, I'm feeling much better, especially after that
delicious feast. I think I'll get up and study for a
while. Later I'll see if I feel well enough to go to my
afternoon class."

"Sounds good, but don't overdo it, pal," Val said as
she tossed Tess' white terry robe onto the bed with
her free hand. "I can always stop by your professor's
office and pick up your assignments."

"Thanks, Val. You're a gift." Tess shuffled into
her slippers.

Val smiled a bittersweet smile. *A gift. No one has
ever called me that before. Not even my mother.* Especially not her mother. Until her late teens, Val had
taken care of her mother—and never once had the

woman uttered a word of thanks or shown a gesture of appreciation. Val felt an acute sense of loss spreading through her stomach like ice. "Thanks, Tess," she said softly, her voice barely above a whisper.

"Thanks for what?" Tess looked up in surprise as she tied her robe around her. "You're the one who deserves gratitude."

"What I mean is. . .thanks for saying thanks." Val bit her lip and looked away, a terrible tenseness seizing her body.

Tess sat in silence for a moment, studying Val thoughtfully. "I mean it," Tess said, tilting her head, her shoulder-length black hair glistening like polished ebony in the soft light filtering through the window blinds. "You _are_ a gift, and I'm glad we're roommates."

Val turned quickly and scurried down the hallway so Tess wouldn't see the pain dancing across her features.

ช

The stove clock read 7:20 A.M. as Val finished washing the last of the breakfast dishes. She'd showered and dressed quickly, pulling on jeans and her new navy KSU sweatshirt. She'd dragged a brush through her thick chestnut hair and even spared thirty seconds for a sweep of mascara and a hint of shadow to bring out the jade in her eyes.

Now she was running late. If she didn't hit the pavement by 7:35, she'd be late for Investigative Journalism at eight o'clock. And tardiness wasn't something Professor Weston took kindly to.

I haven't even made my lunch yet, she groaned to herself. *I shouldn't have talked to Tess for so long.* But she had to admit to herself that wild animals couldn't have torn her away until she'd heard every word of Joel Bennigan's remarkable conversion.

Somehow, even as Val watched the clock tick away precious minutes, she couldn't seem to get going. She lingered with her hands in the sudsy, lemony-smelling water, thinking about what she'd just learned.

Joel's a man whose life has been marred with pain, yet he exudes such joyful confidence in God's providence, she thought as the ran her fingers through the soft bubbles. *I've stomached pain too—but I don't have that trusting faith. . .why? What's wrong with me?*

She wanted to know more about this man and his faith—the reason behind that intense conviction in his voice and the passion in those clear blue eyes.

Her reverie was interrupted by the ringing of the telephone. She started and jumped backward, splashing herself and the immediate area with soapy water.

"I'll get it, Tess," she called out as she grabbed for the kitchen towel. The receiver almost slipped out of her still-wet hands.

"Hello. . .Val?" said a rich masculine voice.

Her heart lurched. "Yes?"

"I hope I'm not calling too early. This is Joel Bennigan."

Val swallowed hard. *It couldn't be.*

"Val. . .are you still there?"

"Y—yes, Joel." Val took a deep breath and squared

her slight shoulders. "Good morning. This is a surprise." Her mouth felt dry despite her efforts to sound confident. She was thankful that Joel couldn't see her white-knuckled grip on the receiver.

"I apologize for the hour, but I wanted to catch you before you left for class," he hurried on, excitement edging his voice. "Kevin Milford finally saw the truth about the Children of Last Days Light last night!"

"Oh, thank God!"

"Amen to that. And thanks for your prayers, Val. I needed them," said Joel, his voice warm and soft. "Last night was a spiritual battle for Kevin's soul. We talked until four o'clock this morning."

"Wow!"

"It was a close call, I tell you. Another week of brainwashing and I don't think I could have reached him."

Val blinked in disbelief. "Oh, Joel. It sounds so frightening! How can these groups brainwash people right here in the United States—in the name of religion?"

"The Evil One comes to steal, kill, and destroy, Val," Joel answered somberly. "As Christians, our war is not against flesh and blood, even though the devil uses flesh-and-blood cult leaders to enslave God's children. But the Lord Himself warned us that false prophets would come in His name and deceive many."

Val fell silent for a moment, absorbing the powerful implication of what Joel was saying. "Well, I have a lot to learn about cults."

"Hey, no sweat!" said Joel, his tone suddenly

lightening. "Bennigan to the rescue. I've got at least half-a-dozen books I'd be happy to loan you—plus an earful of my professional opinions!"

"Sounds like an offer I can't refuse, Reverend Bennigan."

"OK. How about lunch at Brady's? That's the coffee house on Main Street next to the campus. It's a popular student hangout and they serve the best coffee in the Midwest."

A date? Is he asking me for a date? Val willed her voice to remain steady. "Sounds great, especially since I don't have time to make a sandwich," she retorted.

"Oops! Sorry to have held you up, Val. To make amends, lunch is my treat. . .agreed?"

"Agreed."

"Then we're on. I've been hoping for the opportunity to get better acquainted."

Val thought she identified something more than pastoral interest or Welcome Wagon politeness in Joel's voice . . .at least, she hoped she did. Could he be attracted to her as she was to him? She felt a heady sense of both excitement and alarm.

"I'll look forward to it," she said, trying not to appear too eager. "Say at noon?"

"Noon it is."

"I'd better run now," Val said, "or I'll be late for another important date—with Professor Clive Weston, the Bear of KSU's journalism department."

four

Val scribbled frantically as Dr. Weston paced back and forth in front of the blackboard, his professorial tweed jacket perfectly complementing his brown suede shoes and heavy cotton twill pants.

"Personal ethics and public responsibilities," he intoned, pausing long enough to print both phrases on the aging green board. He stepped back and flecked the chalk dust off his jacket, grimacing in annoyance.

"What is the press's responsibility?" His dark eyes glared over the bifocals perched on his ample nose. "Does a man's—or woman's—personal ethics impinge on that person's public life? Is it the duty of the press to report any breach of personal ethics?

"Why, in my days of covering presidential campaigns, we turned a deaf ear to any rumor of a candidate's mistress," he continued, positioning himself in front of his fifteen graduate students. "Everyone knew it and no one reported it. Back then, we stuck to reporting only a president's public activities. A man's private life was his own, not to be invaded by the curious." Weston paused and stroked his graying beard.

The pale light streaming through the high, narrow windows cast a hazy halo around the professor as he stood alone like a performer on stage, the dreaded Bear who could humiliate with a word or ruin a grade with the flip of a pen. "Whose business is it anyway if a public servant is indiscreet in his personal life? How is the public's interest damaged?" he challenged.

The long-haired young man who sat beside Val let out a low chuckle and raised his hand. "You're right, Dr. Weston," he piped up in an insolent tone. "Who are we to pass judgment? It's no one's beeswax what an elected official does privately. . .not as long as he or she is performing the elected duties satisfactorily." A self-satisfied smile spread slowly over his long, thin face, showing small, yellowish teeth.

"Is that so?" Weston raised a bushy eyebrow and scanned the room for opposition. "So your position, Mr. Hardy, is that one's personal code of ethics has no bearing on public life?"

"That's right. What I do in my spare time is no one's business but my own," Hardy said, his reedy voice gaining confidence. "No one's perfect. Anyway, it's a free country." His metal chair scraped across the tiled floor as he scooted back to plunk his boots on the desk in a triumphant gesture.

Val cast a sidelong glance at Phillip Hardy, tilted back in his chair, hands defiantly laced behind his head. She'd often found herself put off by the young man's swaggering attitude, his cigarette smoking, and his belligerent tone of voice.

She glanced around at her classmates. A few nodded in assent. Several looked bored—as if the answer was so obvious that the question itself was inane. Most had worked for newspapers and news magazines for several years. Most, like Val, were in their late twenties, but unlike her, most of them denied faith in a personal God. Val knew she didn't fit the typical industry profile—politically liberal and religiously agnostic. But she was also aware of her responsibilities as a Christian to make gospel values known in a secular environment.

She cleared her throat and raised her hand. "I disagree, Dr. Weston."

"Go on, Miss Packard."

Val willed her heart to stop hammering. "Personal ethics cannot be separated from public life," she began. "Human beings are integral, whole beings. We cannot compartmentalize ourselves.

"If a man is dishonest in his private life—say he cheats on his wife—that lack of personal ethics will show up in his public life. Sooner or later, he'll cheat on the taxpayers, too."

"Noteworthy, Miss Packard," Weston grunted. "So you're saying that public servants should be held accountable to a higher law that prescribes a code of personal ethics?"

"Yes. That's exactly what I'm saying."

"And whose law might that be?"

"The law of the Creator. The Bible originally guided our judicial system." Val swallowed hard and took a deep breath. Already Phillip Hardy was rolling his eyes and throwing angry glances her way. But she wasn't through. "It should continue to guide those entrusted with the public good."

"So you would deny the validity of Mr. Hardy's

conclusion?" Weston probed.

"Yes, sir, I do."

"What?" Hardy screeched, jumping to his feet, causing the metal chair to hit the floor with a tremendous clang. "This is religious oppression—pure and simple! Keep your God's laws out of my personal life, you . . .*you religious fanatic!*"

Val clutched the side of her desk and stood up to face her adversary. "Mr. Hardy, the last time I read the Constitution, I believe it said 'freedom *of* religion' not 'freedom *from* religion,'" she said quietly, but firmly. "Our founding fathers never meant to wipe religion out of public life."

Hardy's lean face flushed purple with rage. "You Christians are all the same—trying to force your religion on everyone else," he sputtered. "Well, I tell you, it won't work! I, for one, intend to do what I please! Read what I please!"

Val found herself trembling in the presence of the man's rage. She had always hated confrontations of any kind. She felt her face flush. The blood began to pound in her temples. Quickly, she sat down, careful to avoid Hardy's withering stare.

"Eh, Mr. Hardy, I think you've made your point," Weston interjected. "You may sit down."

Weston directed his next question to Val. "Aren't your standards a little. . .narrow. . .for today's world, Miss Packard?"

"I suppose so, but at least they're challenging," she conceded, looking the professor straight in the eye. "But challenges both create and demonstrate character, and don't we need people of character in public service?"

Several students shifted uneasily. Hardy sat fuming.

"Hmm. . .well, let's move on, class," Weston announced, not bothering to address Val's point any further. "You need to begin your investigative projects this week."

He paused for a moment, then turned again toward Val. "Miss Packard, since you have an interest in religious topics, why don't you investigate our local cult?"

"You mean the Children of Last Days Light?"

"Exactly. They claim to be Christians who do good. Detractors say they're charlatans. Perhaps you could find out the truth."

Val sensed a sincerity in Weston's gruff challenge— perhaps he was offering her a chance to save professional face after the run-in with Hardy. And she couldn't deny that the incident with Kevin Milford had aroused her interest in cults. Plus, Joel would make a good resource person.

"I agree, sir. I think it would make an interesting project," she said after only a moment's hesitation. "I'll do it."

"Good," Weston said shortly and shuffled some papers on his desk.

Hardy scowled. "Right. That is, if you can live in the real world long enough to write a story."

"Mr. Hardy—please! I demand civility in my classroom," Weston barked. With that, he snapped his attendance book shut, straightened his red knit tie, and strode out of the room.

"Yeah. A Christian capable of an unbiased investigation," Hardy sneered. "And pigs can fly."

❧

Val cut across the grassy campus and arrived at Brady's a few minutes early, her ego still smarting from Phillip Hardy's rude manner. As she pushed through the swinging wooden doors, the satisfying smell of exotic coffees welcomed her and buoyed her flagging spirits.

She inhaled deeply and smiled. Joel had good taste. Quickly she scanned the room crowded with college students, but could spy no tawny mane.

The heels of her leather boots clicked smartly on the bare wooden floor as Val picked her way to a booth at the back of the shop. The dark, rough wood interior had the feel of an Old West saloon right out of a movie set. But instead of wanted posters, there were pictures of literary artists and musicians, announcements of poetry readings, and flyers proclaiming a series of jazz concerts jamming the walls. One entire wall was lined with coffee mugs of all shapes and sizes. *I wonder what all that's about,* Val thought. *I'll have to ask Joel.*

She checked her watch. 11:50 A.M. She glanced around again, a little rattled by the eagerness with which she was looking forward to seeing Joel.

What if he doesn't show? Maybe I should leave. . . Oh, don't be such a wimp, Val Packard! Her thoughts ran in circles, nipping at each other's heels like a pack of stray dogs. She tried to quiet her nerves by studying the menu written on a chalkboard behind the counter.

"Mocha Java, Colombian Dark, Cinnamon Espresso," a deep voice beside her boomed. "Yes, Val, Brady's is truly a coffee-lover's paradise."

Val swung around and, for the second time in as many days, found herself staring into the handsome face of Joel Bennigan.

His eyebrows arched mischievously. "What'll it be, Val? French Roast or the House Special?"

"Oh, Joel! You startled me! How nice to see you."

"Likewise. You're a sight for sore eyes after a night of arguing against cult indoctrination." He pulled off his brown leather jacket and slung it over a chair.

"Well, my investigative journalism class this morning wasn't exactly a picnic at the beach," Val said. Suddenly, she found her eyes misting over and desperately tried to swallow the hard lump in her throat.

"Hey, Val pal, what's the matter?" Joel slipped in beside her on the booth bench and put a strong arm around her shoulders.

"Oh, nothing much. At least, nothing I should feel upset about." Val bit her lower lip. "Just some angry fallout from a fellow student who's got a thing against Christians."

"Tell me about it." Joel gingerly reached over to wipe away a tear stealing down Val's cheek. "What happened?"

"Well, Phillip Hardy raged at me in front of the entire class when I spoke up in defense of personal ethics and accountability in public life," she said in a pained voice.

"Oh, I gotcha. The old 'Christians-imposing-their-values' line?"

"Yes," Val sniffed. "He even had the nerve to call me a religious fanatic!" She winced at the memory. "I was so embarrassed."

Joel stroked his chin. "Hmm. . .Phillip Hardy. The name rings a bell. But why?" He frowned in thought. Then his face darkened. "Oh, yeah. Now I remember. He wrote a string of nasty letters to the editor, condemning the local churches for speaking out against pornography in the bookstore."

"Oh, no wonder he despises Christians," said Val. "Now his attack makes sense."

"C'm here, Val." Joel squeezed her shoulders, then reached into his knapsack. "Let me offer you a few words of comfort."

He drew out his Bible, opened to the New Testament, and read, his voice as rich as velvet: "'Blessed are those who are persecuted for righteousness' sake, for theirs is the kingdom of heaven. . .pray for those who. . .persecute you' (Matt. 5:10, 44).

"The Lord warned us about the Hardys of this world," Joel went on. "If we're standing up for the gospel, we'll be persecuted. It's a given. Including the tongue-lashing Hardy dished out this morning."

Joel's words felt like a cooling hand on a feverish forehead. Val sighed and released the tension she'd been storing in her muscles ever since the confrontation. "Thanks. That helps me put the incident in perspective." Suddenly, she felt much better.

"And what's more," Joel continued as he slid his Bible back into his knapsack, "the Bennigans are living proof that Christian ethics and public life do go together."

"Oh?"

"Sure. My family have been landowners and politicians in Kent for well over a hundred years. A couple of my forefathers served as mayors. We've had city council members in the family—even a state senator back in the thirties. All were committed Christians and all served the public well."

"Well, thanks for telling me," said Val with a smile. "That gives me some ammunition for the next time I'm attacked."

"Standing up to Hardy was courageous, very courageous," said Joel. There was a look of undisguised admiration on his face. "I'm proud to know you."

"Thank you," murmured Val. She was glad the dim lighting hid her flushed cheeks.

"Enough maudlin behavior—I want food!" Joel jumped to his full six-foot-three stature. "What'll it be? I recommend Brady's Reuben sandwich, to be washed down by a robust cup of Mocha Java."

"I trust your good judgment, Reverend Bennigan."

From her cubby-hole, Val watched Joel's every movement as he ordered lunch at the counter. His large body moved with the agility of a lion, his toned physique betraying his former life as a football star. The rich outline of his shoulders straining against the fabric of his shirt caused Val's pulse to quicken. She looked away quickly in case he caught her admiring gaze.

"Here you are, pretty lady," he crooned as he placed a steaming plate of corned beef and sauerkraut on toasted rye in front of her. "Best lunch in Kent."

"Thanks, Joel. This is a treat."

"My pleasure, ma'am. Think nothing of it." He asked the blessing then took a huge bite of his sandwich.

"One thing I've got to know," Val announced seriously, her face dead pan. "What's with all the mugs on the wall? There must be at least a hundred!"

"Oh, that's Brady's way of making you feel at home," Joel said. "The coffee aficionado can house his or her favorite mug on the wall and use it whenever visiting this fine establishment."

"What a grand idea!" Val clapped her hands. "I love it. It's so homey."

"I think you'll find Kent's a pretty homey town."

"Well, tomorrow I'm going to bring my favorite mug and ensconce it with its cousins," she decided.

"I've been meaning to do that myself," said Joel. "Remind me, will you?"

"Sure. But how come your handsome mug—so to speak—isn't on the wall already? Didn't you eat here during your college days?" Val bit into her sandwich, her mouth puckering a little from the tartness of the sauerkraut.

"Oh, yes, the glories of my bygone football career," Joel said, grimacing. "Back then, my beverage of choice came in a beer mug, not a coffee cup. I was a self-satisfied star in my own game. . .until I found the real Star."

"That's quite a story."

"Yep. It just goes to prove that God never gives up on anyone." Joel took a sip of coffee. "Ahh. . .now that's good! No, like the Hound of Heaven, God kept pursuing me into the bars and down the football fields of my life until I could accept His gift of grace."

"Like Paul."

Joel looked at her over the rim of his cup. "I suppose I've got a lot in common with our brother Paul. We both knew that all the success in the world can't bring salvation. Only the love of God can do that."

"I wish I could be as sure," confessed Val after a brief silence. "Somehow, I never feel that I quite measure up. . .even with God."

"That's just it, Val," Joel said, putting down his sandwich, his eyes suddenly serious. "We don't have to measure up. Scripture says that while we were yet sinners, Christ died for us. Having to earn God's love—or measuring up—is a delusion.

"In fact, that's one of the favorite lies of the Children of Last Days Light and their leader, Father Elijah."

"I'd be interested in knowing more about them," said Val, eager to to steer the conversation away from her spiritual shortcomings. "I'm writing a paper about the cult for class."

Joel fished around in his bag again and pulled out four hardback books. "Here's the best research available on cults and mind-control," he said, handing them to Val.

"Cults manipulate through guilt, fear, and intimidation," he went on to explain. "They target people having a tough time—a freshman at college, someone getting over a broken romance. They come on super strong with love and affection. But it's just a sales technique.

"Once they get a person on a weekend retreat, they use sleep and food deprivation, indoctrination, manipulation—you name it—to get control of that person's mind."

Val put down her fork and stared at Joel in amazement. "Since no one in their right mind would join a cult, these groups manipulate people into joining?"

"Exactly." Joel nodded. "Cults are religious rackets, each run by a competent con-man to satisfy his lust for power, money, and, often, sexual conquest. Or anger. Like Father Elijah, a defrocked minister with a chip on his shoulder the size of Ohio."

"Well, I want to learn more—and quickly," said Val. "I want to give Weston the best piece of investigative journalism he's ever seen. I'll show him Christians can do the job."

"Attagirl!" Joel said with a grin. But Val thought she discerned more than admiration for her stand in his glance.

"Reverend Joel!" A young man's voice shattered the intimate moment.

Joel rose as a thin youth with closely cropped dark hair barreled toward their table. "Kevin! Hey, buddy, what's wrong?"

five

Kevin Milford practically threw himself into the booth beside Joel. His eyes looked wild and he was gasping for breath as if he'd been running.

"Whoa, Kev. Who's after you? All the demons of hell?" Joel asked, half-joking until he saw the anguish flooding the young man's features.

"Maybe! I think I'm in big trouble! I—I'm afraid I've lost my soul!" The smooth, freckled face crumpled like a paper cup, and he buried his face in his hands.

"Hold on! Let's talk about this."

The concern in Joel's voice seemed to soothe Kevin. He raised his tear-filled eyes to the big man.

"What happened, Kev? Did they contact you?"

"No. And I've stayed away from them, just like you said," Kevin whispered, his voice breaking. "But I was just reading my Bible, and some of Father Elijah's teachings came back to me—the ones about how God would punish, even kill anyone who left the group. And how backsliders were committing the 'unforgivable sin' against the Holy Spirit and would lose their salvation. I went to the church and they told me I could find you here."

Joel frowned and put his arm around Kevin's shaking shoulders. "It's not unusual that you're recalling some of the cult teachings. It's a type of post-traumatic stress. What verse?" With his free hand, Joel reached for his Bible.

"Second Thessalonians 2:11."

Joel found the reference and read, his tone authoritative yet gentle: "'Because they received not the love of the truth, . . . God shall send them strong delusion, that they should believe a lie; That they all might be damned who believe not the truth.'"

Joel snapped his Bible shut. His lips thinned. "I'm sick to death of Father Elijah twisting the Word of God to frighten people," he said sharply, his voice edged with aggravation. "I'll bet I can tell you exactly how he misused this verse."

Kevin's eyes grew wide as Joel continued, "He said that if you—or anyone else—left the group, you'd be turning your back on the truth. Therefore, God would punish you. He'd delude your mind. He'd let you believe a lie because that's all you'd deserve as a backslider."

Kevin nodded.

"So, according to Father Elijah, God is the Great Deceiver and you'd never know if you did the right thing." Joel spat out the words in disgust. "It's a ploy to terrorize you into staying with them. A diabolical ploy." He tightened his grip on Kevin's shoulder.

The young man slumped in despair. "How'd ya know?" he asked, his eyes downcast.

"I know how they use fear," Joel said, compassion softening his strong features. "And I know that God doesn't operate that way."

When Kevin looked up, Joel's eyes leveled with his. "God doesn't terrorize us, Kev. He doesn't deceive us. He guides us like a father. He respects our freedom to make mistakes and helps us pick up the pieces afterwards. . . . Here, let me buy you lunch, and we'll read through that entire chapter to see what it really says." Joel turned to Val. "Would you like to read along?"

She nodded, and Kevin looked at her in surprise, almost as if he hadn't noticed her before.

Val stretched out her hand. "I'm Val Packard. I'm learning all I can about cults for a class paper," she said as she clasped Kevin's clammy hand.

"I'll tell you my story, if it'll help," Kevin offered. "But one thing I know for sure—I could never have gotten free of them if it hadn't been for this good shepherd." He inclined his head toward Joel.

Surprise, then delight, crossed Joel's features. "Just doin' my job, folks," he said, jumping to his feet. "What'll it be, Kev? A Reuben or a grilled cheese? It's on me."

❧

Over the next month or so, Val never missed Joel's Bible study or the Sunday service. She came to look forward to his odd phone call asking how her research was going and if she were settling in. A few times, they met at Brady's for lunch.

When Reverend Tillman, the senior pastor, preached, Joel sat in the pew with her and Tess. As he held their hymnbook, bellowing out the sacred songs in his slightly off-key voice, Val felt herself drawn into a more joyful worship than she'd ever known. Even so, the few times she and members of Joel's family had attended the same service, Val had managed to avoid them. With her background—the kind of home life she had known—she had been afraid they would disapprove of her. Surely they'd see right through her. It was a fear she couldn't seem to shake.

On Saturdays, Val began helping Joel as he transported the not-so-fresh produce from Bennigan's Groceries to the homeless shelters in Kent and nearby Ravenna and Akron. She watched him chop carrots in the shelter kitchen with a wino, read a bedtime story to a homeless kid while her mom scoured the paper for work, and plan a fund-raiser with the new shelter director.

Not surprisingly, Val knew she was growing fonder of Joel Bennigan every day. His laugh was infectious; his wit, quick and sometimes as dry as kindling wood; his strong presence, reassuring as he they walked along the banks of the peaceful Cuyahoga River, treading a path through the cathedral-high trees, ablaze with the reds and golds of autumn.

Once they took a day trip in his Blazer. *He obviously enjoys driving,* Val noted as he sped skillfully along the winding country roads. They crossed the rolling hills of southern Ohio, soft and billowing like a sheet in the wind, dotted with cattle and sheep.

"Ohio is a beautiful state," she murmured.

He nodded. "Ohio, the heart of it all," he said, echoing a popular radio jingle.

They stopped for lunch at a small country inn. As

they wolfed down large omelettes stuffed with Amish Swiss cheese and ham, they tossed jibes back and forth and generally enjoyed each other's company.

Afterwards, while they lingered for hours over a pot of hazelnut-flavored coffee, Joel chatted about growing up in Kent. Val poured out her dreams of becoming a top-notch journalist. It seemed that they never ran out of things to talk about, no matter how much time they spent together.

Suddenly, a look of mischief sparked Joel's China blue eyes. "Val, my journalistic pal, there's something I've wanted to ask you all day. Let me take you away from all this!" He gestured dramatically around the charming inn with its Amish quilts lining the walls, hand-hewn oak furniture, and a roaring fire in the antique iron grate.

Val was puzzled. "Why? What's wrong with this place? It's lovely."

Joel blinked, looking around as if seeing the room for the first time. Then he cleared his throat. "So it is. But come with me anyway. Come home with me to meet my mother!"

"Meet your mother?" Val's eyes widened in surprise. What was he talking about? Wasn't that something one did if one's intentions were. . .serious?

Laughter rumbled deep in Joel's chest. "Val—you don't know my mom. She'll love you! You'll love her! She cooks a huge family dinner every Sunday afternoon. Please come."

"Oh, Joel. I don't know. . . ." Whatever he meant by this unexpected invitation, Val wasn't ready. Meeting his family was the last thing she wanted to do. What if they didn't like her?

"Please be our guest this Sunday, Val," he said. "All joking aside, I'd be honored. I think you'd enjoy my family—all seven kids, a couple of spouses and a splattering of grandchildren—not forgetting Ruthie, my foster sister."

Val was overwhelmed by the sheer size of his family. "All those children. . .and your mom takes in a foster child as well?"

"That's Millie Bennigan for you," said Joel with obvious pride and affection. "Now that the youngest Bennigan is a teenager, she decided she needed someone else to mother. Ruthie's ten years old and was born severely disabled. She can't walk or talk or even feed herself."

Val shook her head in sympathy. "How awful." *So that's why he invited me home with him. His family is accustomed to taking in strays.*

"The poor girl lived in an institution until two years ago, when my mother got her hands on her. Millie thinks disabled kids can make great additions to families."

"Millie sounds wonderful."

"Mom's a godly woman," said Joel, as he drained the last of his coffee. "I, for one, wish I'd listened to her wisdom earlier in my life. My dad's great, too. And I think you'd get along with my sister Charity."

Suddenly, like a flash storm on a summer afternoon, old insecurities engulfed Val. Childhood fears of not being wanted, not being adequate. She thought she'd walked away from them when her mother died, but they'd found her again, even in this remote country inn in southern Ohio. They always found her, sooner or later.

"I'd be intruding. . . I wouldn't want to impose." She shook her head, hoping he'd forget the idea.

"*Intruding?*" Joel's voice rose in disbelief.

"Well . . . it's just that, in my family, visitors weren't always welcome." Val swallowed hard. *If only you knew, Joel. Visitors were never wanted. Even I wasn't wanted. Not after Dad died.*

"You're always welcome in our house," Joel said, puzzlement and concern lining his features. "Honestly, Mom would be miffed if I didn't invite you."

"Are you sure?"

"I am." Joel scribbled the address on a napkin, then thought better of it. "Better still, I'll pick you up."

"I'd rather drive myself." *That way, if I bomb I can leave early.*

"All right. Here's the address. We live ten miles outside town in an old farmhouse on Edison Road. My apartment is in the basement. We're not farmers anymore, though. More like country squires," he said with a low chuckle. "Anyway, you can't miss the miles of white fences—they keep the horses from running away from home. Dinner starts around one, about an hour after church."

"Sure thing. I'll be there," she said, a little too casually.

Avoiding Joel's eyes, Val took the napkin and slipped it into her purse. She tried to hide the awkwardness that suffused her—the feeling of not belonging, of never being wanted or loved. *If my own mother couldn't stand to have me around, what makes me think anyone else would? Even the Bennigans.*

"You're sure I won't be a bother?" she asked again, her voice almost a whisper, her downcast eyes wide with vulnerability.

Her question was so soft that Joel almost didn't catch it. "Hey, friend, why so skittish? I can't believe this! You're brave enough to stand up to the likes of Phillip Hardy, yet you're quaking in your boots over a dinner invitation? Yes, we want you there. Trust me. I wouldn't lie to you."

He frowned thoughtfully, then smiled a soft, sad smile. "Whoever gave you the message you weren't wanted? All I can say is, it was their loss."

Val closed her eyes against the tears that threatened to expose her. Desperately, she tried to quell the struggle that raged within. Should she reveal her hidden scars? Joel Bennigan was, after all, proving himself to be a dependable friend. Instantly, the old responses kicked in. *Hide. Deny. Just like always. Don't trust. Don't feel. Don't talk. You'll get hurt.*

She shook her head, as if to shake off the old oppressive rules she'd lived by for so long. She took a deep breath, blinked, and opened her eyes, only to find herself staring into the incredibly kind gaze of Joel Bennigan—blue pools of life, pain, and unquenchable warmth.

"Val, we *want* you there. Talk to me. Don't shut me out."

She pushed down the lump that had formed in her throat and smiled weakly. His eyes told her she could trust him. She wanted to. Like a timid swimmer testing the water with one toe, she threw out a single nugget of personal information. "I didn't have a happy childhood, Joel. Not like you."

"I've been incredibly blessed, I know, but you—you're not to blame for a lousy childhood. No child is."

"I don't know. Somehow, I always felt things were my fault."

"What things?"

"Oh. . .my father's death in Vietnam, my mother becoming the town drunk. . .her death, despite all I tried to do for her. . . ."

"Val—those things were beyond your control."

Val pressed on, before she lost her nerve. "My mother not wanting me. . . ." Her voice trailed off into a husky whisper. "I always felt that if I could be better, do more, get better grades, be a perfect child . . .my mother would have loved me."

The ugly memory of her childhood loneliness and shame threatened to undo her fragile composure. She wished she could take back the revelation and toss it, along with her long hair, over her shoulder as if she didn't have a care in the world. But it was too late for pretending. At least with Joel Bennigan.

She breathed deeply, waiting for the inevitable feeling of being judged—the feelings she'd grown up with. The scornful stares and clucking tongues. She waited. It didn't happen.

Instead, Joel took her hand and squeezed it. "Maybe she wasn't capable of love, Val." His voice was low and full of comfort. "Maybe alcoholism crippled her ability to cherish you. But that doesn't mean no one wants you now."

"I'd like to believe that, Joel. I really would."

Joel hesitated slightly. "I know what I'm talking about, Val," he said slowly. "I had a close call with drinking myself, during my college days. It can take over your life. No one, nothing else matters."

"You?"

"Yes, I was on my way to becoming an alcoholic when I got hurt."

"Oh—I didn't know. . . ."

"After I turned to the Lord, I got counseling and went to Alcoholics Anonymous meetings for a while. I met many people there who had neglected their children emotionally—not out of lack of love, but because of their addiction."

He squeezed her hand again and a wistfulness stole into his expression. "So, you see, not being loved wasn't your fault."

Val could feel her throat closing up. "I want to believe you," she whispered.

"Try. Ask the Lord to help you." He hesitated, measuring her for a moment, and then eased into a smile. "Ask for the grace to help you believe in His love and the love of your brothers and sisters in Christ. Take the first step by accepting my invitation. . . please."

Something leaped up in Val's heart. Some feminine

need to be taken care of, to trust, to be cherished. Her instincts told her she could believe this man of God. Trust wouldn't come easy, but she'd try. With God's help, she'd try.

As she silently searched his brilliant blue eyes, she felt a fragile sense of connection growing between them, an empathy that was slowly but surely weaving them together. She felt a faint glow of happiness spread throughout her body.

"You *do* understand, don't you?" she said at last. It was more an observation than a question.

Joel nodded gravely. "I think I do."

She sat up and straightened her shoulders. For a few long moments she stared wordlessly at Joel, her heart pounding. She licked her lips nervously. Then she spoke. "I—I'd love to come to dinner and meet your family, Joel Bennigan."

A new and unexpected sense of self-confidence surged through her. She felt as light as air.

The smile that flooded his face was her reward. "Way to go, Val! This is gonna be a Sunday you'll never forget!"

six

Later that evening, Joel stopped in at Brady's. He badly needed time to think. Time without distractions of any kind.

He sat alone, nursing a half-cold cup of coffee in his favorite booth at the back of the shop. The population of the coffeehouse had thinned considerably since the dinner hour, and the waitresses were busying themselves, wiping down the wooden tables in preparation for the evening poetry reading.

Joel knew he should be getting home. Early in the morning, he had hospital calls to make. Still, he sat in the empty booth, transfixed by the memory of this woman who'd swept into his life so unexpectedly six weeks ago. Val Packard both attracted and puzzled him.

His hands tightened around his ceramic mug. Was this romantic attraction he was feeling for her? For the first time, he admitted the possibility that his feelings for Val were heading into a dangerous zone. As a minister—a young, single minister—he knew his responsibility not to show partiality to any parishioner. Especially any beautiful, single female parishioner.

Taking a sip of the lukewarm beverage, Joel resolved to limit his feelings for Val to pastoral concern. And, as her pastor, he *was* concerned. Why was she so scared? At least, that's how she'd looked when he'd asked her to meet his family. Haunted and lonely. Frightened like a doe unnerved by a back-firing car. But why?

Why would a beautiful woman like Val be intimidated by an invitation to a family dinner? And her self-confessed lack of confidence in God's grace—where did that come from? Yet, like a true soldier of Christ, she hadn't lacked the courage to speak up to the likes of Phillip Hardy. Joel shook his head.

Val's plight might not have bothered him so much except that he knew some of those painful feelings. Knew them all too well. Feelings of inadequacy. Of futility. All the posturing and machismo bravado of his former football life came rushing back. The emptiness of it all—the insecurity, the longing. He knew Val's pain, all right. Intimately.

Try as he might, he couldn't get her gentle green eyes out of his mind. A man couldn't forget those eyes. Almond-shaped and gold-green, like sun-tipped dark green summer leaves. And hair the color of a setting autumn sun, cascading down the slight shoulders she squared with such determination when she felt threatened.

Spunk and vulnerability. Val had both. And that baffled him. It made him want to wrap his arms around her protectively, all the while praising her gumption. He shook his head again, as if to clear it of the powerful emotions that shook him. If he could just get his hands on that person who had hurt her so badly. . . .

Before he realized it, Joel found himself balling his

right fist and slapping it into his cupped left hand. Flames of anger licked at the edge of his consciousness.

Then he caught himself. *Ah, angry again, Bennigan? When are you going to put away the old man and try Christ's way of dealing with things for a change?*

He sighed and put his hands flat on the table. Under the table, he stretched out his long, well-muscled legs and willed his body to relax. *Take it easy, guy. Don't you remember: "Be angry and sin not"? The anger of man works not the righteousness of God. When are you going to learn that? Jesus got mad in the temple, but he never punched out anyone's lights.*

He was falling for her, all right. Woman of contradictions or not, Val Packard was stealing his heart. This fierce, primitive, bewildering desire he felt for her—he hadn't felt that way about a woman in many years, not since he'd turned his life over to the lordship of Jesus Christ nearly a decade ago.

He took a swig of cold coffee. The ache to hold Val and soothe away her hurt swelled inside his chest, gripping his heart, tightening his throat.

Since his conversion, he'd been careful about his personal life. He'd concentrated on seminary studies. Then he'd thrown himself fully into the ministry. That old unwritten law about ministers not playing favorites with parishioners had made it easy to keep his distance from the female members of the congregation. The Lord's work kept him busy, too busy for a personal relationship with a woman. And for a long time, the ministry alone had been enough.

But lately, he'd felt a restlessness. A yearning. Especially when he presided at a wedding and witnessed the love of a man and woman for each other. He ached for a love of his own. For a partner in Christ.

Now there was Val. *Dear Lord, please use me to help heal her suffering. Whoever and whatever has hurt her so deeply, let me bring her comfort.*

Joel flinched at the self-serving tone of his prayer. He knew he wasn't praying for Val's healing alone. Resisting the urge to dictate to God, he shrugged his shoulders. *OK, OK. You know best, Lord. Thy will be done.*

ع

The Indian summer sunshine filtering through the giant silver birches dappled the private road leading to the Bennigan estate. And when Val drove up to the huge, well-preserved stone farmhouse, it, too, basked in the pools of buttery light splashing across the neatly trimmed grass.

A couple of toddlers' big-wheel bikes lay strewn on the wide front porch. A new Buick, a gleaming black Taurus, and a red mini-van lined the curved driveway in front of the house. Val imagined a cozy family gathering inside the old homestead, and that thought made her shudder.

I knew this was a mistake. I shouldn't have let Joel talk me into this. Her heart sank as though weighed down with cement blocks. She cast about for a place to turn her car around. Why risk more rejection and disappointment?

Then she saw Joel tearing up the driveway in an old green Pontiac, obviously in need of a new muffler. He braked right behind her. When she caught his broad, grinning face in her rearview mirror, her nervousness evaporated.

"Hey, Val! Want to race?"

She tried to suppress a laugh. "To where—the junkyard?"

"Hey, hey, no fair denigrating these worthy workhorses." He jumped out of his wreck and strode over to Val's. "Like faithful old horses, they deserve nurturing in their old age."

"Ah, so the church's Car Ministry could be more accurately described as an old jalopy farm?"

"Come see for yourself." Joel opened her creaky door and bowed with a mock flourish. "Just walk this way, m'lady, and I'll show you Faith Bible's hospital for sick cars."

Val followed as Joel rounded the sculptured bushes flanking the side of the house. She breathed deeply of the fresh country air tinged with the musty smells of fall.

The Bennigans' pastures and woods—no doubt, Bennigan land—stretched as far as the eye could see. Out back stood a large, four-car garage, obviously a later addition to the property. With a jerk, Joel threw open one of the wooden doors to reveal an old pickup mounted on bricks.

"Meet this tired old nag," he said, patting a faded green fender. "Ever since Pat McKinley lost his job when his tire company moved out of Akron, his family's seen hard times."

Val nodded. She'd read the McKinley name in the prayer corner of the church bulletin.

"He earns much less now that he's working for a tree care company in Kent, and his wife can't work at all because of her lupus," Joel continued. "On top of everything, they have five kids. Pat's been hauling light freight in Old Betsy here, but he can't afford the maintenance anymore. That's where our Car Ministry can help."

Val was impressed. "This ministry shows God's love in such a practical way."

"Our God is a practical God," Joel said matter-of-factly as he opened the hood and checked the fan belt. "Jesus was pretty down-to-earth when He multiplied the loaves and fishes—a very practical solution for a bunch of hungry people.

"In fact, ignoring physical needs and spiritualizing everything—like the Children of Last Days Light does—is not the gospel of Christ."

The reference to the cult piqued Val's curiosity. "What do you mean by 'spiritualizing' everything?"

"It's cult doctrine—not only the CLDL, but any of the thousands of destructive cults across our country," Joel said as he closed the hood, a heavy thud reverberating through the dark, dusty wooden building.

"They say only the spiritual is good. The physical is evil. That line of reasoning ultimately denies the incarnation of Christ. After all, if matter is evil, why would God become human? And, if the flesh is evil,

why take care of it? Never mind that Christ made
lunch for the multitude. Cults like the CLDL deny
their members medical care and proper nutrition.
That's what I call 'spiritualizing' everything."

Joel reached up to pull the garage door down, as
Val stepped out into the bright sunlight. "Tell me more
about the cult. This is fascinating."

"Well, a couple of years ago, a CLDL member in
Kent nearly went into a diabetic coma because the
cult forced her to throw away her insulin."

"What?"

"If you have faith—according to their teachings—
you can throw away all your medication—even eye-
glasses. Illness is totally spiritual, and any man-made
intervention—insulin, for example—is evil. Medical
attention is pandering to the flesh. A lack of faith."

Joel slammed the garage door, and they started up
the red brick pathway toward the house.

"Unbelievable!" Val fell into step. "What happened
to the girl?"

"She collapsed on Main Street and a passerby called
an ambulance. The hospital notified her parents, who
came down from Cleveland and brought an ex-cult
member to talk to her. Thank God, when she recovered, she was able to go home. She's one of the lucky
ones."

"What do you mean?" Shocked at what she was
hearing, Val stopped dead in her tracks.

"Haven't you heard, Val? Kids have died in these
groups," Joel said quietly as he came to a halt beside
her. "Others have been so wounded psychologically

that they need extensive professional and spiritual help when—and if—they leave."

Val shuddered. "It's sinister."

Joel studied her face for a moment, started to say something else, then seemed to think better of it. Suddenly he reached out, gently touched her forearm, and smiled. "Hey, listen, I'm sorry to put a damper on the day. This is our special Sunday, remember?

"Let's just enjoy ourselves. We'll talk cults later. Right now, Mom's in the kitchen preparing a feast. The table is set, and all the cups are running over."

"Quit twisting the Scriptures to your own destruction, bud!" Val quipped as she punched him playfully on the arm.

"That's the cult's job. It's my job to gather you in for the feast," he retorted as he chased a breathless Val up the winding path to the back door.

seven

"Mom, I'd like you to meet Val Packard, a graduate student in the KSU journalism department and the next Barbara Walters."

Millie Bennigan stood at her white ceramic sink peeling potatoes. The sunlight streaming in through the wide windows suffused the large country kitchen in a yellowish glow.

"Oh, Joel!" Val waved away his compliment.

"So pleased to meet you, my dear." Mrs. Bennigan's plump hands clasped Val's. A warm smile lit up her motherly, lined face as a wisp of gray hair escaped from the hair knotted inot a bun at the back of her head. "Journalism is a noble calling for a Christian."

"I think so too, Mrs. Bennigan."

"Please, call me Millie. 'Mrs. Bennigan' makes me feel, well . . . so *old*."

"Ma, you're one of the youngest people I know," said Joel, bending down to hug his mother. "Short, maybe, but not old."

"Scoot, son, before I make you peel these potatoes. How about giving me some time to get acquainted with Val here?"

"All right, Ma. I'll give that old Pontiac a quick checkup."

"More Car Ministry?"

"It belongs to a widow who needs transportation to work tomorrow."

"All right, son. But don't get too dirty. Dinner will be ready soon."

"Right, Ma. Whatever you say, Ma. Your wish is my command, Ma. . . ."

"And don't you call me *Ma!*"

Joel dodged the deftly aimed swat of Millie's dish-cloth as he bounded out of the kitchen. Val couldn't help chuckling and wondered why on earth she'd been afraid of the Bennigan family.

"That's my boy," sighed Millie. "So full of fun." A tiny frown marred the smooth brow. "He wasn't always like that, though."

"You mean. . .his football days?"

"Yes," she said with another heavy sigh. "There wasn't a day that I didn't beg the Lord to bring my son into His fold. Who would have thought that terrible accident could be the start of a whole new life?"

"'God draws straight with crooked lines,'" Val said, remembering her roommate's words.

"Never a truer saying, my dear. But let me introduce you to the rest of my brood. Then we'll get going on these spuds."

Val found herself shepherded out of Mrs. Bennigan's kitchen with its yellow flowered wallpaper through a pair of massive sliding golden oak doors into a huge, noisy living room. Sprawled on a thick, pale green Oriental rug were several adults and children engrossed in a game of Candyland.

Two stunning young women—identical twins with

long, tawny hair—sat on a green leather couch, polishing some silverware and laughing uproariously at a private joke. A dark-haired girl snoozed in her wheelchair, her frail limbs folded in upon her crooked, wizened body like an accordion.

The soothing strains of contemporary gospel music—from a stereo somewhere in the room—filled the air. Val marveled at the simple elegance of the antique furnishings, especially the hunter green velvet Queen Anne chairs and the fine white marble fireplace.

"The house was built in the 1880s," Mrs. Bennigan said when she noticed Val's admiring glances. Then, raising her voice over the din, the matriarch made the introductions.

"Val, over yonder is my second son, Matthew, with his wife, Sarah, and my two grandchildren, Petey and Andrew. And this is my oldest girl, Charity. Ruthie seems to be taking a nap—although how she can sleep with this racket, I don't know. But then, she's hard of hearing. And, of course, this is my husband, Robert."

The Candyland crowd paused in their play, and the adults leaped up to welcome Val. Matthew pumped her hand. Sarah smiled. Charity piped in, "We're so glad to meet you. Been at KSU long?"

"Just since the beginning of the semester," Val replied, instantly liking the tall dark-haired woman, who appeared to be about her own age.

"Now don't be a stranger," Charity replied. "Maybe you can find a little bit of home here on the Bennigan ranch—and lots of down-home cooking, thanks to my mom."

Robert Bennigan lowered his pipe from his mouth and nodded. His salt-and-pepper hair and heavy mustache gave him the appearance of a movie star of the Cary Grant vintage. "Delighted to meet you, young lady."

Now I know where Joel gets his good looks and charm, Val thought. She smiled her gratitude and, following Mrs. Bennigan's lead, turned her attention to the twins.

"And these two complete the family," she said fondly, nodding toward the two girls. "May I introduce Faith and Hope."

Val caught herself chuckling at the interesting trio of names, realizing that the three girls bore the names of the three great Christian virtues.

"Mom—no more jokes about our names," one of the twins pouted good-naturedly as she set down her work to hug Val. "Joel told us he'd invited you to dinner. But you're even prettier than he said."

Val blinked in surprise, her heart racing at the thought of Joel's flattering description. *Maybe this attraction isn't so one-sided, after all,* she thought. Impulsively, she hugged Faith and clasped Hope's outstretched hand. "Thank you for welcoming me into your home," she said honestly.

For the first time since her father's death, Val felt surrounded by love and allowed herself to sink into the warm comfort of the Bennigans' emotional embrace. *I want a family like this. I want love like this.*

"And thank you for coming," said Mrs. Bennigan as she steered Val back into the kitchen. "Now, let's get going, my dear. Those spuds aren't going to peel themselves."

As they worked, Val learned that the Bennigans had originally left Scotland in the 1870's to work on the Kent railway. Unlike many immigrants of that time, the three Bennigan brothers had arrived with a little money and, after the railroad opened, they became farmers, hacking their homestead out of the wilderness.

"Back then, the family owned a right sizable chunk of land—close to two thousand acres," said Mrs. Bennigan as she plopped another sleek, peeled potato into a large cast-iron kettle. "They raised cattle and horses and a lot of the crops and produce. Around the turn of the century, they opened the first dry goods store in Kent. They also supplied grain for the Quaker Oats company in Akron.

"Over the years, most of the land was sold off to developers. All we have left is this hundred acres. No more cattle either—just a few pleasure horses. Later generations of Bennigans chose to concentrate on the grocery business instead of farming."

"I'm impressed, Millie," said Val, well aware of the prosperous chain of Bennigan Groceries that stretched across Ohio. "A real American success story."

Mrs. Bennigan nodded, causing yet another strand of hair to escape from her bun. "Yes, indeed. Other family members have gotten into politics and, of course, church work. Joel's not the first Bennigan minister, y'know," she said pertly, pride lacing her rich contralto voice. "Our family helped found Faith Bible over a century ago."

The woman fell silent for a moment, lost in thought. "Yes, the Lord has mightily blessed my family," she said as she tossed the last potato into the huge iron pot. "And you, dear? What about *you?* I've been hogging the conversation all this time, blowing our horn, and haven't asked a thing about your family. Do forgive me!"

"Not at all. You have such a fascinating story." Val frowned slightly and shrugged. "I just wish I knew more about my own roots. I have a few relatives in California and an uncle who used to visit before he moved to Florida. But Dad was killed in Vietnam . . .and my mother passed away a couple of years ago."

There was a look of utter sympathy on the older woman's plump face. "Oh my dear, I'm so dreadfully sorry."

Val pretended to be absorbed in drying her hands. She blinked back the tears that misted her eyes.

Mrs. Bennigan quickly changed the subject. "May I confide in you, dear?" she asked as she leaned her broad frame toward Val, her hands splayed. "It's about Joel."

Val caught her breath. "J—Joel?" she stammered in bewilderment. "What about him?"

Mrs. Bennigan placed her hands squarely on Val's shoulders. "That boy of mine is so lonely, it just breaks my heart."

"Lonely? Joel?"

"Oh, he hides it well. He's so devoted to the Lord's work that he doesn't give himself five minutes to realize he's lonely. But I know. I can see it in his eyes when he watches our lovebirds, Matthew and Sarah."

"Oh." A soft gasp escaped Val's lips as her mouth dropped open. This was a side of Joel Bennigan she hadn't suspected. She narrowed her gaze. Why was his mother telling *her* this?

"What he needs, my dear, is the companionship of a good Christian woman. Someone like yourself. So why don't you slip on out to that garage and see if that boy of ours needs some help?"

The older woman winked mischievously. "And tell him dinner will be ready in forty-five minutes—and not to be late!"

Speechless, Val could only nod. Then she snapped her body around and hurried out the back door. *She thinks I'm good enough for her son! If only she knew who I really am—Val Packard, daughter of the town drunk—she'd warn Joel to run a country mile.* Val shook her head in disbelief as she wound down the path toward the open garage door.

Stepping inside, it took a few seconds for her eyes to adjust to the dim light inside the musty building.

At her approach, Joel stopped tinkering on the Pontiac's engine, straightened up, and turned to face her. "Orders from the boss?"

"Sort of. Dinner in forty-five minutes. In the meantime, I'm to see if I can help you." Val shrugged her shoulders and held out her arms in a helpless gesture.

"I know how to drive my car to a garage when it needs fixing. But that's about the extent of my car repair repertoire."

Joel eyed Val with mock seriousness and scratched his chin. "Hmm. . . Carburetors—want to take a whirl at learning to fix one? Or how about transmissions? Or maybe you'd like to try your hand at replacing a fan belt?"

She made a face at him. "You know I'm hopeless! My talents lie in other areas, Joel Bennigan."

"I'm well aware of that, Miss Packard. Then perhaps you could exercise your talent by handing me that wrench."

She obliged, and he ducked his head under the raised hood. "Give me a minute, Val. I'm nearly finished here. Just another twist. . .ah, there we go. Another minor mechanical miracle for the Car Ministry." He slammed the hood shut. "Now c'mon and let me show you around the old homestead."

Joel slipped off his green coveralls, revealing tan corduroy pants and a crew-knit pale blue sweater beneath. He grabbed his denim jacket from a hook on the back of the door as he strode outside, pausing for a moment to wash his hands under the garage faucet.

"We-ell," Val began dubiously, "just as long as we're not late for dinner. Millie's orders."

"I'd trade forty-minutes with you for all the exotic coffee in Brady's."

"You joker!" Val punched his arm.

"You think I'm joking? Val, you're better than a blend of Mocha Java, Espresso, and the Brady house special!"

They laughed together, but a glint of seriousness smoldered in Joel's eyes. Val saw it and her pulse quickened. He slipped his arm around her shoulders and guided her toward the woods beyond the pasture.

"Where are we going?" she asked.

"Down by the lake. If we're lucky, we might see a few deer."

They walked a couple of hundred yards before reaching a clutch of red-sided barns that hugged the line where pasture became woodland. A horse whinnied as they passed.

"That's Jasper," said Joel. "Charity used to show horses. But not anymore. Now we just keep a few old favorites for ourselves and the disabled kids from Manor Farm. Horseback riding is an amazingly good therapy."

"Manor Farm?"

"Sorry, Val. I forget how new you are to Kent. Especially since it seems I've known you all my life." Joel flashed her a grin. "Manor Farm is a home for mentally retarded children."

"And horseback riding is good for them?"

"Yes. At least for the higher functioning kids."

"That's news to me." She fell silent. *I could do with some therapy myself about now.* In Joel's powerful, masculine presence, she found herself increasingly self-conscious and insecure.

Looking down at her pants, she fretted. Maybe the red ones would have been more flattering. And what about her makeup? Had it smeared? Was her conversation witty enough? What on earth did Joel Bennigan see in her anyway?

Her mind flew back to a time when she had never felt insecure, when she had been her daddy's "little princess." For the first eight years of Val's life, Marc Packard had showered his only daughter with attention. She had felt pretty and self-confident and happy. The world had been at her feet as long as Daddy had been at her side.

"You have the softest, most beautiful hair, Princess," Marc Packard said as he braided seven-year-old Val's hair for school.

"Daddy, where's Mommy? Why doesn't she ever braid my hair like you do?"

"Oh, your mommy's just a little tired. Hurry up now or you'll be late."

"OK, Daddy." Val puckered her lips for a kiss as her father handed her the lunch he'd prepared.

"Your favorite, Princess. Cheese and ham with a special pickle, orange juice, and a brownie."

"Thank you, Daddy," she squealed in delight. "You're the best daddy in the whole wide world and I love you!"

"And I love you too. And don't you ever forget that—not even for a minute. You're my princess and that makes you the prettiest, smartest girl ever."

Val hugged her father and skipped outside to catch the school bus. Somehow, it didn't bother her too much that her mother was never around. At least, not as long as she had Daddy.

Val had learned as a toddler not to bother Mommy. She was always tired or sick. Dad was the one who soothed scraped knees and hurt feelings.

But then Daddy went away to a big, grown-up fight in a country far, far away. He sent black-and-white photographs of himself in nasty camouflage clothes, wearing a helmet and carrying a gun. He said he was counting the hours until he saw her again.

Then a strange man knocked at the door and told them that her daddy was dead. Her mother cried like a wounded animal and fled to her bedroom, leaving Val alone with that terrible word. Dead. Her daddy wouldn't be coming home anymore.

Val sat on the couch for hours, her back straight and her small shoulders squared, trying not to cry. She had to be brave. Now that Daddy was gone, Mommy had no one to take care of her. No one except Val.

She tiptoed up the stairs to listen at her mother's door. From inside came the sound of muffled sobs and the clink of glass. Only a door separated her and her mother, but it might as well have been a continent.

In the years that followed, Val learned to take care of her mother—to walk her home from bars, to put her to bed when she passed out, to make excuses to neighbors and bill collectors. She always tried to smile and pretend nothing was wrong, but people knew. Everyone knew. Townspeople in the supermarket stared as Val did the grocery shopping. She saw them shake their heads.

Kids at school called Joan Packard the town drunk, even to Val's face. No one wanted to be friends with Val. There were no slumber parties, trips to the mall, or girlish secrets for her. No boyfriends either. No boy in his right mind wanted to be seen with the daughter of a drunk. . . .

eight

For a while, Val and Joel walked without talking. The only sounds came from the brittle twigs snapping beneath their feet and the lonely cooing of a dove calling for his mate.

Val's brooding was interrupted by the sight of the man-made lake, large as a football field, nestled beyond the woods. She caught her breath at the magnificence of its flat expanse of water, mirroring the silver span of sky.

The water held a small wooden ship in its liquid grasp—a toy obviously forgotten by one of the grandchildren back in the house. Val imagined happy family times around this lake—picnics, swimming, fishing, children playing. The kind of times she had never been able to hoard in her own memory.

"It's beautiful," she said softly, almost reverently.

"Yes, it is," said Joel as he slipped off his jacket and spread it on a patch of grass near the water. "This was where I came to think as a child. My special place. A kid in a large family doesn't have many private places.

"Come, sit down," he invited, patting his jacket. "But we've got to whisper if we want to see any deer."

Val eased herself down, thankful that she'd chosen comfortable lightweight slacks. But her knit top proved a tad light for the coolish breeze, and she wished she'd worn her jacket. She was glad for the warm nearness of Joel's body. He sat, arms curled around his long lean legs, gazing intently at the lake.

Plop! Plop!

"What was that?" asked Val, a little startled.

"Oh, just the Bennigan frogs. They hide in the long grass around the water and, when some crazed notion seizes them, they fling themselves into the water."

The plop of diving frogs, the prickle of pine needles, the occasional lazy lap of water stirred by a breeze, and the faint spice of Joel's aftershave all indelibly etched themselves onto Val's senses.

"'Season of mists and mellow fruitfulness. . .'" Joel's rich baritone filled in the comfortable silence.

"'Close bosom-friend of the maturing sun,'" she added. "John Keats, if my memory serves me correctly."

"You're right. Keats," he said, a wistful smile tugging at the corner of his mouth. "The poet of romantic love."

He swiveled his torso and looked at her, a spark of indefinable emotion in his eyes. "Do you believe in romantic love, Val?"

"I—I don't know. I'd like to. . . . What I mean is, I've never met the right guy. . .I suppose."

"Maybe we can change that," he said deliberately, his eyes never leaving her flushed face.

Val drew in a sharp breath. *He can't mean what I think he means.* Quickly, she looked away, her heart pounding. Her eyes narrowed as she focused her gaze on a pair of ducks swimming lazily in the middle of the pond. She stiffened her back. *But I won't let myself be hurt.*

"Why, Val?"

"Why. . . what?" Had he read her thoughts?

"Why are you so afraid? You're young. You're beautiful. You're fun to be with. These past six weeks have been the best in my life. You've got the guts to battle the spirit of this age in Weston's classroom, but in your personal life, you're scared. You're afraid to let anyone get too close. Specifically—me."

"How do you know all this?" she asked defensively, still refusing to look at him.

"I recognize the pain you carry around. I've carried my share, too," he said softly as he curved his fingers under her chin and tilted her face toward his. "I care about you. Let me help you unload that burden. Trust me."

Val's words stuck in her throat. Warmth suffused her body as Joel's eyes held her captive. She breathed deeply, savoring the hint of musky masculinity that was his alone. Then in one swift, gentle movement, he lowered his mouth to hers and brushed her lips with a kiss so soft and tender, tears formed behind her closed eyelids. She felt weak as he gathered her to himself and she went into his arms willingly.

"It grieves me to see you in such pain," he said softly. "It grieves God, too." He stroked her hair tenderly. It felt as soft and silky as he had imagined.

Joel could feel her heart beating wildly against his chest, like the heart of a wounded deer. She reminded him of a hurt doe he'd found in these woods when he was a youngster. She'd been torn badly by barbed wire, but he'd nursed her back to health.

As he held Val, Joel tried to absorb her hurts, to soak them into himself. He could feel her trembling. At that moment, he would have given anything to take away the emotional pain that hobbled her. But he knew he couldn't. Not alone, anyway.

"Val, please, honey. . . ."

He felt her stiffen. Quick as a startled animal, she pulled away from him, her eyes flashing with angry hurt. "Don't you mock me, Joel Bennigan!"

"Mock you?" Joel spread his hands in a gesture of helplessness. Val jumped to her feet. "A man like you could have any woman he wanted. Why are you toying with my emotions?" She spun sharply on her heel and began to walk away.

"Toying? Mocking? In two long strides, Joel was beside her. He grabbed her by the shoulders. "Whatever you're thinking, Val, it's all wrong. I care about you."

"No man cares about the daughter of the town drunk," she said quietly, dropping her eyes. "Go get yourself someone better. Someone you won't be ashamed of. Do it now. You will anyway. So don't expect me to wait around for the inevitable."

Joel cupped her face in his hands. "But I want you, Val. I've wanted you from the night I met you. . .just as you are. You're not the daughter of a drunk. You're Val Packard. A wonderful, funny, brave, and vulnerable woman—and I'm falling in love with you."

Wonderful. . .brave. . .funny? He was falling in love with her? Joel's words echoed inside Val's head, ricocheting around like bullets in a tin can, almost deafening in their implication. "You can't possibly mean that. You can do so much better." Her heart hammered against her ribs. Even now, she could hear her mother's taunts: *You're no good. No one will ever love you.* A knot rose in her throat.

"Val, don't put yourself down."

Joel's thumb gently brushed away the tears that slipped down her cheek. Her skin felt soft and cold. His heart ached for her. She looked so desolate.

He watched her eyes as they darted back and forth, as if searching his face for something. *Deceit? Honesty?* Joel saw a shy yearning in those soft green eyes. A guileless confession that she found him attractive. He doubted—no, he *knew*—that she hadn't intended for him to see that. But he did. And he would honor and protect that vulnerability. Always.

"You're God's child, Val. Made in His image. His daughter—think of it!—worthy of dignity and respect. So loved that Christ died for you."

His words were soft, but full of passion. His eyes never left hers. "You're worthy of being wanted, Val, even by a klutz like me. I'm so sorry if my kiss caused you to panic. I never meant to hurt you."

His eyes were so full of tenderness, Val found herself slipping under his spell, beginning to believe, to trust. She swallowed with difficulty and found her voice. "You really mean that, don't you?"

"More than anything in the world. Be my lady, Val."

With a pang, she realized that he was waiting for her reply. The choice was hers, completely. She could take a risk—right now—and open her heart to love, or slam that door shut and continue to exist in her wintry world of loneliness.

Everything within her wanted to scream yes. Now. Before it was too late. *Dear Lord, help me.* Realizing for the first time that she was shaking, she took a deep breath and tried to relax. "Yes, Joel. Yes."

The words rushed forth like a tremendous sigh, and the tension drained from her body. The heavy lump in her stomach disappeared, and a wave of warm relief flowed through her.

"Thank you, thank you, thank you." Joel's eyes glazed with tears as he crushed her to his chest and reclaimed her lips. His kiss was full of tender possessiveness and protection. He caressed her face, trailing kisses down her cheek. "Val, my gal pal," he whispered in her ear. She saw a smile spark in his eyes and light up his face. "You've made me so happy . . .so very happy. We're going to be wonderful for each other, I promise you."

He pulled away slightly, his hands still clasping her shoulders. Slowly, with delight, his eyes scanned her face. "But right now we'd better get back to the house before we make my mother very unhappy."

She nodded, too choked up for words.

He scooped up his jacket, draped it around Val, and wrapped his arm around her shoulders. She snuggled against him as they strolled toward the house, drinking in the pure comfort and exhilaration of the bond that was forming between them. Her heart ached with happiness.

"Look—Val—deer!" Joel whispered urgently.

He stopped dead in his tracks and put a finger up to his lips. Sure enough, a family of deer had meandered up to the lake for a drink. Two adults and a young fawn took turns drinking.

"A papa deer, a mama deer, and a baby deer," Joel said softly, tightening his grip around her shoulders. "A family, Val. God's answer to loneliness—for the deer, and for us."

nine

"Infiltrate the cult?" Joel dropped his fork onto Val's kitchen table with a loud clatter that made her jump. "You can't be serious?"

"Of course I am. What better way to get the inside scoop—the real story?"

"But. . .to *infiltrate?* Val, don't you know how dangerous that could be?"

"Weston challenged me to find out the truth," she explained. "I want to do the best job possible."

In the pale midday sun filtering through her cream café curtains, Val saw alarm flash across Joel's face. His presence dominated her tiny kitchen. His denim jeans and a burgundy cotton pullover buttoned at the throat made him look more like a lumberjack than a pastor of souls.

She sighed. She hadn't anticipated disagreement. "My plan is to let them recruit me—temporarily, of course—and play along with their game for a couple of weeks."

Joel shook his head. "It's not that easy," he said. "These guys are racketeers."

Val's heart sank. In the week since their special moments at the Bennigan homestead, they'd grown so close. Conflict was the last thing she wanted. *But then, I knew it was too good to last.*

"Do you think I can't pull it off? That I'm not a competent journalist?" She bit down hard on her lower lip to stem her disappointment.

"No, no. This isn't about your competence. Not at all. Those newspaper clips of yours were great, really great." Joel reached across the table and closed his hand over hers. "But cults are dangerous, Val. It's not like writing a feature story on the Christian Women's Club."

"I know that, silly," she retorted, trying to lighten the tension that had spoiled their lunch. "I've studied those books you lent me. I understand how cults operate—mind manipulation through fear, guilt, sleep deprivation. . . ."

"Why put yourself at risk?" he interjected.

"To research a paper that'll knock the socks off Weston and show Hardy that Christians can do good work, that's why," she replied with a toss of her head. The grim line of Joel's mouth told her he wasn't convinced.

Val was sorry she'd brought the subject up. "Listen, I love the fact that you want to protect me," she bumbled on unhappily. "I really do, Big Fellow. But I'm a grown woman and I can take care of myself. Besides, forewarned is forearmed—and I know so much about this group that I'm armed to the teeth!"

"*Big Fellow,*" he echoed with an unexpected chuckle. "Where on earth did you come up with *that* name?"

"Michael Collins—Irish hero, big man—like you. Led the Irish fight for freedom in the early part of this century. I read about him in one of my historical romances."

"Ah, I see. So I'm your hero?"

"You might say that." She blushed furiously at this revelation of her romantic daydreams.

"Glad to be of service," he replied, grinning and dipping his head in a mock bow. Then his face darkened again. "But I don't want to have to lead a campaign to win your freedom from the CLDL."

Val shrugged, slipped her hand out of his, and picked up her tuna fish sandwich again. "I think you're exaggerating the danger. I really do."

"But, Val, they use brainwashing techniques. Who knows what the pressure is like once they really get their claws into you? They may use the name of Christ, but they twist the Scriptures for their own purposes."

He reached across the table and tenderly traced the contours of her chin and jaw. His fingers felt warm and gentle. She almost relented. Almost.

"I just don't want to lose you, Val. You've no idea how much you mean to me."

Her mouth twisted wryly. She still couldn't believe—really, truly believe—that Joel Bennigan loved her. Joel came from a respectable family. Every feminine instinct told her he'd never commit to an intimate relationship with a woman who had grown up as the daughter of the town drunk. *Like mother like daughter, they say. He'll come to his senses. It's only a matter of time.*

"Joel, it's just a research project, nothing more. It'll be all over in a few weeks." She sighed, resigning herself to the prospect that her relationship with Joel would probably be over even sooner.

"I still don't like it," he said, his sandy brows furrowing in another frown. "But if they start pulling you in, I'm going to pull you out. They're not going to steal my lady."

Val laughed self-consciously. "Really, Joel, they're not going to hoodwink me. I know too much. But thank you for worrying, Big Fellow."

⁂

Shifting uncomfortably on a wooden bench outside the sprawling red brick Student Center, Val found the prospect of turning herself into live bait for cult recruiters less and less appealing.

She glanced at Joel. His attention was riveted on the students milling around the plaza as he searched for CLDL members. His stony expression told her he still didn't like her plan, but his presence here was proof that he would support her anyway.

The October wind whipping across the spacious brick and concrete plaza chilled Val to the bone. She felt dwarfed by the gray twelve-story university library towering to her right. The only thing that brightened her mood was watching two of Kent's black squirrels scurrying across the flower beds, dodging the yellow mums and late-blooming marigolds.

She found herself wishing she were sipping coffee at Brady's, or peeling potatoes with Mrs. Bennigan, or snuggling in Joel's arms. There were a million things—preferably centered around Joel Bennigan—that she'd rather be doing.

"Don't look now," Joel whispered. "They've just arrived."

Following the direction of his nod, Val stole a sidelong glance. Two women, both dressed smartly in
mid-calf-length skirts, bright tops, and sensible san-
dals, dismounted from their bicycles. Their hair was
long, but neatly brushed, and they wore no makeup.
Immediately they started handing out pamphlets to
students.

Funny, they don't look like cultists, Val thought.
They look pretty normal to me.

"They're not what they appear to be," Joel whispered urgently, as if reading her mind. "They look
sweet, but they're deadly. Remember it's Father Elijah you're tangling with—not these young women."

Val recalled a magazine photo of Father Elijah—a
tall, sinister man with beady eyes and flowing white
beard. This shadowy figure directed the group through
rambling, vitriolic epistles called "Love Letters."
Parents of cult members called him the devil incar-
nate.

Thinking about Joel's words, Val narrowed her eyes
and watched the women work the lunch crowd streaming out of the campus fast food joint. She felt sure the
key to understanding the CLDL lay in unearthing information about Father Elijah.

Sighing, she strengthened her resolve. *I've got to
get to the bottom of this.* Quickly, she squeezed Joel's
hand, stood up, and crossed the plaza toward the two
women. But she took care not to walk assertively.
Having read that recruiters were trained to spot the
vulnerable, she hunched her shoulders and kept her
eyes downcast, assuming a posture of abject depression.

Just as she had expected, one of the women quickly bounded toward her, bubbling with sunny cheerfulness. "This is for you," the slight redhead chirped, thrusting a pamphlet into Val's hand.

"Oh. . .t—thank you!" Val smiled weakly. She scanned the two pages of closely-spaced type peppered with cartoons. "Who are you representing?"

"We're God's messengers of love," the girl said brightly, flashing a thousand-watt smile.

"I could sure do with some of that right now," Val said in a tight voice.

"What's the matter?"

"Oh, everything's such a mess," Val continued, keeping her eyes on the ground. *Well, that's not really a lie, not with my insecurity about Joel right now.* "I feel so confused about the direction my life is going. And being new on campus doesn't help."

The woman, whom Val figured to be in her early twenties, seemed genuinely concerned. "Oh, I understand. My life was a complete disaster before I met the Family."

"The Family? Isn't that the Children of Last Days Light?" No sooner were the words out of her mouth than Val wanted to bite her tongue. *Now I've blown it! They won't trust me if they think I know too much.* "Not that I've got anything against the CLDL—I just heard some other students around here call you that."

"No problem. I can explain." The girl's intense brown eyes never left Val's for an instant. "Sometimes we call ourselves the Family because those evil church people spread such vicious lies about us. But we don't have anything to hide. We're just messengers of God's true love. Come and visit our home and learn more."

"Oh, I don't know. Do you really think that would help?"

"Not only do I *think* so, sister—I *know* we have the answers you're looking for!"

"Well, then, I think I'd like to. . .eh, what did you say your name was?"

"I'm Gilead," the young woman replied, tossing her long, straight red hair over her shoulder.

"Gilead? Isn't that a place in the Bible?"

"Yes," she said with a light-hearted laugh. "In the Family we take biblical names because we are new creatures."

"What a great idea. I'm just plain old Val. When can I visit?"

"Come to dinner tonight. Just knock on the front door and ask for me. The address is on the back of the pamphlet."

"I'll see you tonight then, Gilead." Val turned to go, feeling satisfied that she'd accomplished her mission.

"Val?"

"Yes?"

"Remember—we love you!"

The declaration flustered Val, and she didn't know how to reply. "Eh. . .thank you," she stuttered, embarrassed that passersby might have overheard the unusual exchange. "Until tonight."

She hurried across the plaza to meet up with Joel

inside the library. When she caught sight of him—his big frame clad in blue jeans and a green sweatshirt, leaning up against the wall with his arms crossed— the relief she felt surprised her. He opened his arms and she threw herself against his chest.

"Whoa, Val! Take it easy. I'm only flesh and blood." He wrapped his arms around her, and she relaxed into the security of his embrace.

"I'm just glad to see you, Big Fellow. That's all."

"I watched everything through the glass doors. She really thinks you're a likely prospect?"

"Yeah. I'm a lost sheep needing to be found by the messengers of love," Val said with an uneasy laugh. "And I'm going to be found—tonight."

❧

Val's heart thudded as she knocked tentatively on the weathered door. Of all the old wood frame houses lining Oak Street, this one looked the worse for wear. She noted the torn window screens and the peeling yellow paint. Just as she'd expected.

But what she wasn't prepared for was the thunderous welcome of the bearded, heavyset man who answered her knock. "Faith and begorra! 'Tis a wee colleen! 'Tis a wee colleen!" he exclaimed in a distinct Irish accent, his currant-black eyes transfixing her. "I'm Jeremiah."

Before Val knew what had hit her, the man had encased her in a bear hug and dragged her inside. As she stepped into the dark, narrow hallway, at least a dozen young men and women tumbled down the stairs and hung over the rail, chorusing, "Hi! We love you!"

and "Praise the Lord!"

Stunned by this open display of friendliness, Val followed Jeremiah into the living room. The lime green carpet was old and faded, the walls a sickly, pale orange. At one end stood an unused fireplace. Val felt chilly and refused Jeremiah's offer to take her coat. But she was not directed to take a seat, for the only furniture was a rickety wooden stand holding cult literature.

The man who called himself Jeremiah left the room, and Gilead rushed in, brimming with enthusiasm. "We love you! We're so happy you're here!" she exclaimed, her voice pitched high with excitement. She hugged Val as if she were her long-lost sister.

Val disentangled herself and cleared her throat. "I want to learn more about your message of love," she said, knowing that was what Gilead wanted to hear.

"Hallelujah! Another lost sheep for the kingdom!" Gilead shrieked and hugged Val again, then ran excitedly into the hallway and yelled for the others. The room suddenly filled with people hugging Val and shouting ecstatic praises.

Although she cringed with embarrassment, Val secretly relished the attention. *They seem so sincere. So welcoming. Can this all be an act?*

As the crowd dispersed, Gilead sat down on the threadbare carpet beside Val and produced a large photograph album. "Let me introduce you to our Family, sister," she said as she began leafing through page after page of youthful, smiling faces.

"Why are you all so happy?" Val wanted to know.

"Because we've found our true family, God's family," Gilead said sweetly as she squeezed Val's hand. "We're all brothers and sisters here—about two dozen of us—living together to serve the Lord. We have families like this all around the world."

As Val listened, a constant parade of people passed through the hallway and up and down the uncarpeted wooden staircase. The majority were undergraduate age, she noted. A few, including Jeremiah, appeared to be older, maybe in their mid-thirties.

Greetings flew back and forth: "Praise God, brother!" "I love you, sister!" and "Jesus loves you!" Val lost count of the kisses, hugs, and back claps. The atmosphere vibrated with joy. Little by little, she felt herself relaxing and letting down her guard. *They seem so nice. So sincere. How can they be evil?*

"None of our family members work at secular jobs," Gilead continued. "We spend our days spreading the message of God."

Val was surprised. "How do you provide for yourselves?"

"Oh, the Lord provides for us," Gilead replied quickly. "After all, the Bible tells us not to serve mammon but to pick up our crosses and preach the gospel every day."

"But what if everyone stopped working? How would anyone survive?" Val mustn't let them think she was an easy target.

"Well," Gilead replied confidently, "very few people love God enough to do that. Most Christians are content just to go to church on Sunday. We serve God every day. Do you?"

Her words cut Val like a knife. The CLDL way of life might be unorthodox, but the question was still valid. *Did* she love God enough to devote her entire life to Him?

Val's conscience stung. What was she doing to justify her place in God's family? Yes, she attended church and Bible study. She helped at the homeless shelter. She tried to live a Christian life. . .but that all seemed so inadequate compared with the intense commitment she saw in the eyes of each Family member.

"I'd like to think I love God enough to make any sacrifice He asked of me," said Val thoughtfully. "But I've got to admit, sometimes I wonder if I really am a devoted Christian. . .if I'm good enough to deserve God's love."

At that moment Val was aware of another presence. Swinging around, she found herself face to face with Jeremiah. With his full black beard and long hair, he looked like an Old Testament prophet.

"We are all unworthy sinners," he said, his voice deep and hypnotic. "The least you can do for God is to serve him 100 percent, Val. One hundred percent."

His words tapped a river of hidden guilt somewhere deep inside Val. Was she doing enough for God? She didn't think so.

"I don't know," she offered weakly. "In our church, we run lots of educational and service ministries—like fixing cars for those who can't afford repairs."

"Hmph!" Jeremiah snorted, his disgust obvious. "You call repairing cars 'work for the Lord?' The flesh profits nothing. You're wasting your time. You should be preaching on the streets. The world needs to repent before God metes out his wrath. Already the storm clouds are gathering for the final judgment. We must warn them!"

Val found herself shuddering. Her face flushed and she felt ashamed of herself and of how little she was doing for God. Jeremiah was a big man with a powerful presence. As Val watched, his anger erupted into scalding fury and rancor sharpened his voice. Others passing by in the hall stopped to listen.

"Any Christian worth her salt will do her part," Jeremiah thundered, jabbing a beefy finger in Val's face. "The Lord told Father Elijah that we will be held responsible for each soul that is lost. If we do not give our entire lives to getting out the message, *their blood will be on our hands!*"

He paused, transfixing Val with his flinty gaze. "Any blood on your hands, sister?"

ten

Val hunched over her desk, tucked away in a corner of her bedroom. The amber-tinted computer screen glowed in the small pool of light shed by her desk lamp. Furiously, she typed in notes about the CLDL. Now and again, she glanced toward the window, the black night lapping at the glass her only companion.

By the time Val got home, Tess had already turned in for the night. Val was relieved. Her visit to the cult had hurled her emotions onto a roller-coaster ride. She didn't want anyone—not Tess, and certainly not Joel—to witness her distress. She hardly knew what to make of it herself.

She'd phoned Joel as soon as she returned—as she'd promised—but had kept the call short, begging off by saying she was too tired to talk. She was tired all right. Emotionally spent. All evening, her emotions had ping-ponged. One moment she felt suffused with love and goodwill, the next, guilty and totally unworthy. Now she was dizzy with confusion. Was this group really the work of the devil? Every one seemed so sincere and so completely devoted to God's work. Sincerity and devotion—weren't they good fruits in a believer's life?

And, more to the point, what was *she* doing for God? Precious little. Jeremiah's words "lukewarm Christian" rankled. *Lukewarm Christian. Lukewarm daughter. Defective girlfriend. Always falling short, never good enough.* The story of her life.

Val—wake up! This is a destructive cult, led by a bona fide nut, she reminded herself. *Wolves in sheep's clothing distorting the gospel. Don't let them get to you. Don't be led like a sheep to the slaughter. It's a con game.*

She studied several of the cult pamphlets. "Repent and be saved!" one said. Another commanded: "Forsake all and follow me!" The text underneath read: "We spend our lives preaching the gospel to a dying world. Can you do any less?"

These statements seem so scriptural, Val argued with herself. *But, of course, cults use the Scriptures for their own ends. You can kill a man with the Bible if you hit him over the head with it.*

Still, Val's head reeled. Her palms felt sweaty. Anxiety knotted in her stomach. She typed more notes for her research, carefully documenting the appearance of the house, the type of people living there, and the events of the evening. Weston would be pleased by such attention to detail.

What she didn't record were her feelings of vulnerability in the presence of such open affection and the sense of personal worthlessness and guilt that Jeremiah had stirred up in her soul.

❧

Joel slammed his coffee cup down so sharply that rivulets of scalding brown liquid splashed across Brady's wooden table. Val jumped back in her seat.

"I don't want you to go," he said, bridled anger in his voice. A chill hung on the edge of his words.

Val suddenly felt weak and vulnerable in the face of this new dimension of Joel's personality. She'd never seen him like this before. Her heart hammered. She hadn't expected such a drastic reaction.

"Why? It's only for three days." She broke eye contact and fiddled furiously with her blue mug. "Anyway, I've already agreed to go."

"Val, this is exactly how they win converts—during these isolated brainwashing weekends. Is this so-called retreat at their camp in rural Michigan?"

"Yes." She stiffened. "Why are you so upset? I'm a journalist, Joel. Don't you think I can handle myself like a professional?" She glared at him with reproach.

Joel sighed and shook his head. Then he buried his head in his hands, strong fingers thrust through his hair. "I'm sorry, Val, so sorry. I can't believe I've let my temper get the better of me again," he confessed wearily. "Traits of the old Joel, y'know. The angry 'old man' liked to throw his weight around. Forgive me, Val."

When he lifted his head and looked at her, his Nordic blue eyes were pleading. "I shouldn't tell you what to do. You're not a child. I'm just angry because I'm afraid for you. . .afraid you'll get in over your head."

Val drew in a deep breath. "I have to go, Joel. If I'm pretending to be a new recruit, I've got to go along with the program, and that includes this retreat. Think of the story I'll get."

"It's not worth it," he said, reaching across the table to grab her hand. "Val, you'll be stranded in the middle of nowhere, completely at their mercy. Other journalists have gone undercover and gotten sucked in."

"It won't happen to me," she insisted, tossing back her long mass of chestnut curls. "It can't—I know too much about them. How can they fool me when I know their game?"

"I know you don't want to hear this—but they'll go for your jugular."

Her eyes narrowed. "What do you mean?"

"Your weakest point."

"Which is?" Val had a feeling she wasn't going to like what she was about to hear.

"Your mother, Val. Your alcoholic mother. She did a number on you, even if you can't see it. . .or won't admit it. But you still carry around a lot of guilt about her."

Val bristled and snatched her hand back. She felt as if he'd just branded the words *Reject—Damaged Goods* on her forehead. *Once the daughter of a drunk, always the daughter of a drunk.* The blood began hammering in her temples. She felt her own temper rise.

"H—How could you! How dare you bring that up!" she sputtered, her body stiffening. "If I'm not good enough for you, then why are you wasting your time with me, Joel Bennigan? I'm not a charity case." She bit her lip to quell the tears of indignation. Then her face flushed. "Oh I get it. Maybe I *am*—Case No. 522, just another mixed-up wacko who needs some advice from Dr. Bennigan!"

"Val, you're taking this all wrong. I'm not blaming you for your mother's alcoholism. I'm trying to tell you that cults are experts at using weak spots."

"Well, my mother isn't a 'weak spot.' Not anymore. I'm just fine." Her breathing was ragged.

"At the church, we have Adult Child of Alcoholic meetings, sponsored by a Christian group. Maybe you and I could attend a few sessions. . .just to help you get a handle on the issues. Then you can move on to forgiveness and peace."

"No, thank you. I don't need any meetings," Val replied coldly. "No problems here."

"Val, I love you—but I don't believe you." Joel reached over to cup her face in his palm. She jerked away. "You may believe you buried the problems with your mother, but, honey, you didn't. No matter how much you deny it, your mother's alcoholism wounded you and until you start dealing with that, it's an area the cult can use."

"Poppycock!"

"They exploit weak points—and we all have them, Val—it's not just you." Joel shook his head. "Then they use mind manipulation. Like with Kevin Milford. That glazed-eye look, the disembodied smile, the vacant face that says no one is home. They're out to lunch with Father Elijah."

Val squared her shoulders. "That's not what I see in the Family members," she hissed, her embarrassment turning to raw fury. No way would her wounded pride allow her to agree with him now.

"They put up a good front. . . ."

"I'm going," she interrupted, her voice icy.

"Val, don't go. Please." A muscle flexed in his jaw.

"I'm going . . . and you can't stop me."

His face pale with anger, Joel sprang to his feet. "All right! Throw yourself into the fire! See if I care! I can't take this!"

He stood rigid, his hands balled into fists. For a moment, he glowered at her. Then he snatched his jacket off the back of his chair and barreled out of Brady's without as much as a backward glance. The slam of the heavy door reverberated through the shop like a slap in her face.

Val stared after him blankly, her mouth open. She felt as numb as if she'd plunged into an icy lake. Slowly, she became aware of her fingers and toes again and of the blood racing furiously through her body. Stains of scarlet appeared on her cheeks. Tears blurred her vision. A few students at the other end of the shop gazed at her sympathetically. The young waitress pretended not to notice Joel's explosion.

I knew it wouldn't last. I knew it. I'm defective goods and he might as well have announced it in the Record Courier.

No longer able to control her hurt and anger, Val hung her head and great sobs racked her body. She'd lost him. Just as she'd predicted. She was never good enough. *Never.*

She sniffed and blew her nose. Quickly, she threw a few bills on the table. She had to get out of here.

As she stepped outside the coffee shop into the sharp October wind, one thought echoed in her mind: *Defective*.

❧

Along with everyone else in the room, Val swayed from side to side in time to the music. She noted that the seemingly endless repertoire of folk-style songs accompanied on the guitar had been written by Family members and spoke of God's coming judgment or the blessed status of the CLDL.

Jeremiah and Gilead, both strumming acoustic guitars, motioned the group to clap harder. The raucous singing echoed throughout the uncarpeted and unfurnished wooden lodge. The dozen cabins dotting the CLDL's "Love Camp" in the rugged Upper Peninsula of Michigan had originally been built amid the towering white pines as a church youth camp.

Val felt weary. They had been singing and clapping all morning. The emotional atmosphere in the room now mounted to a fever pitch. Family members flung their arms heavenward and shouted praises. As the session wore on, people grew more and more ecstatic, reaching an emotional peak comparable to a drug-induced high.

Val looked around at the now-familiar faces. She'd spent the last twelve hours with these people. Jeremiah had clearly taken the lead, with Gilead serving as his sidekick and Val's own "spiritual buddy."

Ever since they'd left Kent in the Family's van, Gilead had stuck to Val like cement, talking non-stop, even following her into the rest room. "We don't want you going off by yourself to think and talk to the devil," she'd said with her dazzling grin.

Brother Zebedee, with his carrot-colored curly mop of hair, bobbed his short body in time to the beat. Abinadab, a serious young man with bulbous brown eyes and thinning sandy hair was singing his heart out. They both appeared to be deep in a trance. Val felt as if she, too, were slipping into a trance. The music was hypnotic. Tall, willowy Rebecca smiled incessantly, as did Gilead.

Val surveyed the other "visitors." Susan Hawthorn and John-Joe McGuire—both KSU undergrad students—looked exhausted, struggling to stay alert after only four hours of sleep Friday night on hard, tiny cots in the cold cabins. Elaine Schultz came from Cleveland. Her brother, Ed, had joined CLDL two years previously. "I need to know what's made him so happy," she explained.

They're all genuinely seeking answers. I'm the only fraud, Val thought uncomfortably. *What would they think of me if they knew I was a spy?* With each hour that passed, she felt guiltier about her infiltration. *They're all so sincere—everyone except me.* Familiar feelings of worthlessness swelled inside her. Quickly, she squelched them by throwing herself completely into the songs.

"That was beautiful, brothers and sisters!" boomed Jeremiah. "Are we inspired?"

"Yes!" A roomful of people called out as one.

"Do we love our visitors?"

"Y—E—S!"

"Let's tell them!" Jeremiah yelled, thrusting his guitar in the air.

"We love you—Susan. . .Elaine. . .John-Joe. . .Val!" At that, the Family members descended on the visitors, showering them with hugs and kisses.

Gilead grasped Val's hands between her soft palms. "We *love* you so much, Val," she said. "Welcome home to your true Family!"

"Sharing time," Jeremiah announced, propping his guitar against a wall and motioning the group to sit, legs crossed, in a circle on the bare wooden floor.

Family members obeyed docilely, and the visitors followed their lead. Val was longing for some fresh air and time to herself to collect her thoughts, but she didn't dare break rank. That's how it had been ever since their arrival late last night. All activities were conducted as a group; every minute, scheduled. Privacy was taboo.

"Sharing gives us a chance to get to know each other better," explained Jeremiah. "Some of us have been with the Family for a long time. Some—Rebecca, for instance—are new. This is time for us to tell who we are and how we came here. I'll begin." Val fixed her eyes on the leader's long, untrimmed beard. His shirt was wrinkled, and his jeans were holey. Nevertheless, he exuded an undeniable power.

"Jeremiah is the name Father Elijah gave me," he began. "When I lived in the world—I grew up in Dublin, Ireland—I was a drinker and a biker. A real hellion, to be sure, ridin' my Harley into stores just to frighten them little ol' Irish ladies.

"I was hitchhiking around California when I met Father Elijah. Man, my life changed. I saw the light not long after I set eyes on him. I knew he had the truth—y'know? He *is* the truth! He condemned the churches and their hypocritical ways. He preached total love and dropping out. The old rules don't apply anymore, he said. Only love and Father Elijah. Hallelujah!"

Jeremiah's tone grew sober. "Soon, he will send me to save the lost sheep in Dublin, Ireland."

"Wow!" said Gilead under her breath to Val and Rebecca, her brown eyes large.

"Sister Rebecca," Jeremiah said in a commanding tone, his brows beetling, "share with us."

Rebecca's watery blue eyes darted nervously from one person to another. "I come from Pennsylvania," she began, clearing her throat. "At college, I studied chemistry because that's what my parents wanted. I practiced my parents' religion, too, but I was only going through the motions. It wasn't real. I was empty inside."

She fiddled with a strand of her short, curly black hair. "I was so empty, in fact, that I began drinking. At first, it was just a few beers, then the hard stuff."

Gilead gasped. Her hand flew to her mouth.

"It gets worse," Rebecca went on, her voice trembling. "My boyfriend turned me on to cocaine. By the time I met the Family, I'd dropped out of school. I'm so ashamed to admit this—but I used to steal money to buy drugs. . . from my own parents. Things got so bad. . .I even thought about s—suicide."

The last word caught in her throat. Rebecca's face folded and twisted bitterly. Tears streamed down her cheeks. Val's heart went out to her, and she felt like crying herself. Gilead reached over and hugged Rebecca.

Suddenly, the whole group began to hum. Val recognized the tune—"We Shall Overcome." With arms slung around each other's shoulders, they swayed from side to side. Family members began to weep openly and utter loud prayers in thanks for Rebecca's deliverance.

Composing herself, Rebecca continued. "Th—the Family saved my life. Praise the Lord for our true shepherd. If it weren't for Father Elijah, I'd be dead."

"Amen! Amen, sister," intoned Jeremiah. "So would many of us. Thank God for the true light in these last days."

As abruptly as it had begun, the swaying and humming stopped. Jeremiah's gaze traveled around the circle of eager, open faces, resting at last on Val.

"And what about you, Sister Val? What can you share with your brothers and sisters?"

eleven

"Me—me? Share?" Val gulped.

"Yes," said Jeremiah, his mouth spreading into a thin-lipped smile. "What brought you to the Family?"

Panicked, Val cast about mentally for something to reveal, some innocuous tidbit about herself to throw into the communal pot. Something that sounded sincere enough that they wouldn't suspect her of being the impostor she was.

"Eh. . .I was looking for answers." She wasn't aware that she was holding her breath until it left her lungs in a single whoosh.

She strained to see some hint of acceptance in Jeremiah's face. He had the most hypnotic eyes she'd ever encountered—eyes framed by bushy dark brows. A small scar on the squared-off cheekbones above his full beard gave him a rough appearance, not at all like the other peaceful, guitar-strumming Family members. Jeremiah wasn't an easy man to read. But at six foot three and built like a refrigerator, he was intimidating.

Now he stared at her silently, stealthily, like a big black cat stalking its prey. Inside, Val was squirming.

"Yeah—there aren't many answers out in the world,

are there?" Gilead chimed in.

"No, no there aren't," Val gushed, emboldened by the affirmation. "I was lost, confused, at my wit's end, as a matter of fact. You see, my mother died a couple of years ago. . . ."

"How sad," Jeremiah interrupted. "What took her life?"

"L—liver damage, actually."

"Complications from alcoholism?" His black eyes glinted knowingly.

"Well, alcohol might have had something to do with it," Val conceded hesitantly. "My mother went into a deep depression after Dad was killed in Vietnam."

"And you took care of her?" Jeremiah probed.

"Yes, as a matter of fact, I did. Right up until the end."

"And how did you feel about that?"

"Well—burdened, I suppose," Val replied, picking her words carefully so as not to reveal any vulnerability. "I did what I could to help her. . . ."

Jeremiah seemed pleased. "We understand what a burden you must have carried." The rest of the group murmured their assent.

"So you're an orphan looking for your true family?" he continued, his lips twisting into a cynical smile.

She could only nod miserably.

"Welcome home, sister," everyone chorused, as if on cue. Val's face flushed. She felt oddly warmed by their concern, but also relieved to have passed the "test." They thought she was one of them. She'd outwitted the Family. *Joel would be proud of me.*

What she couldn't understand was the satisfied look on Jeremiah's face.

❧

The group broke for a meager lunch—one Dixie cup of boiled rice and an overripe banana, washed down with raspberry Kool-Aid. They ate outside, even though the weather was too cold for a picnic.

"This isn't much after only one donut for breakfast," Val muttered in dismay as she snapped a squishy, brown banana off a makeshift table.

"We prefer to concentrate on feeding the soul instead of pampering the body," Zebedee replied.

Two hours into the afternoon lectures, Val's stomach rumbled embarrassingly and she was weak with hunger and exhaustion. She lifted her shoulders up and down, then crossed her right hand to massage her left shoulder. She couldn't remember when she'd been so tired—even after pulling all-nighters to finish term papers.

But this was different. The mental stress and unrelenting togetherness aggravated her physical fatigue. Her mind swam from the ceaseless activity. Time began to distort and stretch, like glue oozing from a tube. Had she been here one day or two weeks? It was hard to tell.

This is brutal. I want to leave. But how? The nearest town was fifty miles away. Hitchhiking would be impossible on these deserted roads—if she could even find her way. The camp had no telephone—even if she could work up enough nerve to call Joel and ask him to come and get her. And the only vehicle on the property was the rusty old van Jeremiah had driven from Kent.

She sighed and resigned herself to finishing what she'd begun. *It'll be worth it. I'll show Joel how wrong he was about me. I can stand on my own feet as a competent journalist, no matter what my background.*

At Gilead's disapproving glance, Val stopped rubbing. "Keep your mind on spiritual things, Sister Val," Gilead said under her breath, her big brown puppy-dog eyes wide with innocence. "Aren't you happy to hear the Word of the Lord?"

Val quickly focused her attention on Jeremiah.

"We are living in the end times, brothers and sisters," he bellowed, standing behind a podium at one end of the room. People sat on folding chairs, balancing pen and paper as they took notes.

Val scribbled as best she could. She'd need these notes for her paper. But she was so tired, she found it hard to make much sense out of his talk. The fearful guilt Jeremiah aroused in his listeners was almost palpable.

"You say you love Jesus? Then obey Him! Put Him first." That accusing voice stabbed the air. "God will not tolerate other gods before him—your job, your boss, your family, or loved ones. 'So likewise, whosoever he be of you that forsaketh not all that he hath, he cannot be my disciple.'

"You lukewarm, church hypocrites!" He looked around, scowling at each visitor in turn. "Only the Family is following Jesus full-time, like the twelve disciples did. Come with us and win the world for God! Be one of the chosen few! The end is coming soon—so who needs an education or a job?"

Jeremiah expounded on this theme until the sun went down. He quoted Scriptures. He ranted. Val found herself spacing out, passively absorbing his message, too tired to think critically. She found it increasingly hard to concentrate on anything for more than a few minutes.

To fight this frightening mindless state, Val started counting silently. She'd go to a hundred and then start again. When that proved too difficult, she switched to Mother Goose rhymes.

Once, John-Joe McGuire dared to interrupt Jeremiah with a question about a biblical reference. Jeremiah shot him a scathing look and ordered him to save his questions for later. But the question-and-answer period never came.

After a supper of an orange and more Kool-Aid, Jeremiah grabbed his guitar and the singing and clapping began again, only this time, the songs were punctuated by long sessions of chanting.

"Fa-ther E! Fa-ther E! Who do we love? We love Fa-ther E!" Jeremiah pounded the air with a clenched fist, his followers joining in the motions. Seconds later, Val found herself lost in another dizzying stream of chanting and sweaty hand-holding.

Twenty minutes into the chant, Val felt light-headed and exhilarated. The group seemed to meld together to form one entity. She could no longer hear her own thoughts. After a while, that loss of self didn't matter.

Every fiber of her being was being sucked into the euphoric vortex. An intoxicating frenzy of excitement surged through the room, ending in a crescendo of wild praising.

The chanting lasted well into the night. Even after Jeremiah finally dismissed the group, Val lay awake for hours on her uncomfortable cot, listening to Gilead's snoring. The hypnotic chant kept ringing in her head. She couldn't seem to stop it, no matter how hard she tried. She tried to remember Joel's face, but it kept changing into the face of Jeremiah.

&

The next morning, Val awoke to loud guitar-playing and clapping. She rubbed her eyes and tried to ignore the dry, burning sensation behind them.

"Praise the Lord!" shouted Gilead. "Let's get going for Jesus!"

Val barely had time to yawn before the group careened into the second day of the retreat. She desperately needed time alone to sort out her thoughts. But not a moment of privacy was allowed. Even during an exhausting morning hike through the surrounding pine forest, a Family member paired up with each visitor. She found the ceaseless activity disorienting.

She remembered Joel's warnings about mind control. Maybe she should have listened to him and stayed at home. Then she remembered his accusations about her mother and his angry explosion. She set her jaw. She'd survive this—somehow.

I'll show him I'm not defective, she thought grimly. *If I can't hold onto his love, at least I can excel at my profession. It's all I have left.* She tried to comfort herself with that thought as the group filed into the lodge for the afternoon lecture.

"Fa-ther E! Who do we love? Fa-ther E!"

The chant began again—slow, melodic, rhythmic—and built until the energy in the room reached a fever-high pitch. Val felt it pulsating in waves through her body. She noticed a warm ache in her throat, the liquid in her eyes, and wondered why she was crying. She didn't feel sad at all. She felt empty and absorbent, as hollow as a tube.

Jeremiah led the chant. "We're gonna tear you rookies apart and put you together again the right way—for love! For Father Elijah!" he yelled.

Val felt pressure building inside her head, and a throbbing roar dulled her sense of consciousness. Dimly, she wondered if the Kool-Aid at lunch had been drugged. She didn't feel like herself anymore. She felt as if she existed in a dream world, moving in slow motion through viscous liquid. The only thread anchoring her to reality was the stream of words flowing from Jeremiah's mouth.

She looked around. The Family members all radiated a complete sense of inner fulfillment. *They seem so close to God, yet He seems so distant to me.* The three other visitors looked gaunt and pale and avoided eye contact with her.

"You're wasting your lives studying and working for money," Jeremiah began his lecture, focusing his dark gaze on each visitor in turn. "The Bible says you cannot serve God and mammon. The prophet

Hosea says that he who earns wages, earns them to fill a pocket full of holes."

Val was struck by the fear that all her life, she hadn't been serving God at all. Not really. Not like the Family was doing. She put her pen down.

Jeremiah pounded the podium. "Now that you've heard the truth, you *must* obey or God will strike you down! People who have left the Family have been killed. Some have gone crazy. Who are we to question the Word of God? Follow Father Elijah, lest you be cast into outer darkness!"

Several Family members fell to their knees and began weeping, crying out to God for mercy, and praying feverishly. Over the next ten hours, that fear became a living presence in the room.

"Let each of us confess his secret sin," called Jeremiah. "Perhaps the Lord will forgive!"

Abinabad began a litany of sexual misconduct in his life before he joined the Family. Zebedee followed suit. One by one, each person revealed his or her darkest secret.

Val's heart skipped a beat when Gilead confessed to deserting her alcoholic mother. She shot Gilead a startled look, but the young woman's head was bowed. Her long red hair hid her face, but Val could see from her heaving shoulders that she was crying. *How could she know? Does she know about me?*

Gilead looked up, straight at Val, and whispered through her tears, "It's so simple, so easy. Just let go, Val."

Val stared at her, mouth open. Gilead's tears touched

her. She couldn't understand why, but she did feel like letting go, despite what she knew. It would be easier. So much easier. In this place—removed from everything and everyone she knew—the outside world didn't make sense anymore. She clenched her fists to steady herself. She knew she was losing all perspective.

Maybe I'm selfish. Maybe I'm wrong about the group. Maybe I should let go and forsake all. So Gilead deserted her alcoholic mother. . . .

Val could hear her own mother's piercing voice. She almost looked over her shoulder, half expecting to see Joan Packard's lined, haggard face peering into her own and screeching, "You ruined my life! You're incapable of love. You're a failure as a daughter. No one will ever love you!"

Val shook her head, trying to rid herself of the voice from her past. As her mother had deteriorated, her taunts had grown crueler and her rages more frequent. Although Val tended her night and day, she could never please the older woman.

"I never loved you!" were her mother's final words before she slipped into unconsciousness for the last time.

Val found it difficult to breathe. The pain of those words engulfed her, twisting in her gut like broken glass. She doubled over, sobbing and rocking, her arms folded into her abdomen.

The litany of sins continued, like a continuous drone punctuated by loud tears and wails. When her turn came, Val heard herself confessing her own secret guilt.

"I never did enough for my mother," she cried, her voice cracking with anguish. "I didn't love her enough. I was never good enough. . . ."

The words tumbled out. She couldn't stop them. Maybe if she confessed, forgiveness would come. Waves of anxiety washed over her. She felt emotionally naked. All her normal defenses had been stripped away.

Then Jeremiah's voice boomed above her head. She looked up. His massive frame towered over her, his finger jabbing toward her face. "You failed your mother," he accused. "You failed God. You must atone for your sin."

"How?" she asked weakly, peering up through her tears.

"There's only one way!" he roared. "God is giving you a second chance—right now. Forsake all and join us. It's the only way. If you're obedient, God will take away your guilt. Father Elijah says so."

Val felt as if her whole system was on overload. Inside, she was being dismantled, piece by piece, and she couldn't do anything to stop it. Her thoughts were chaotic. Her mind churned. Pangs of guilt stabbed her stomach.

Suddenly, she found the room unbearably hot. The praying of the others—so deafening a moment ago—now seemed to be coming from a long way off. When had everything become so quiet?

"Take me, Father Elijah, take me!" wailed Zebedee.

"Take me!" cried Elaine and Rebecca in unison.

Val cupped her face in her hands. Her benumbed

brain conjured up Joel's face. His tender, warm smile.
His fingers gently curving under her chin to tilt her
lips toward his. . . .

*Stop! He doesn't love you. He can't love you. You're
unlovable.* She remembered the anger flashing in his
eyes the last time she had seen him. She heard the
slamming of Brady's door as he stalked off. She should
have known it would end that way. *Mother said no
one would ever love me, and she was right.*

Val rocked back and forth on her haunches, eyes
closed, sobs racking her exhausted body. She forgot
about her fear of being exposed. Water streamed down
her face, and a cleansing, cooling river seemed to surge
through her entire body. Tears of release fell in a pool
on the bare boards beneath her.

All the years of pain—all the years of responsibility, guilt, shame, anger, rejection—burst forth in one
uncontrollable baptism. The twenty-year-old dam lay
in ruins. The tidal wave of emotions threatened to
drown her.

Suddenly, she felt a heavy hand shake her shoulder.
She cringed under Jeremiah's accusatory stare.

"God is calling you, sister," he said forcefully.
"Don't fail Him again. Surrender."

Val felt like Alice in Wonderland falling down the
rabbit hole. Her father had often read her that story
at bedtime. She felt as if a huge hole had suddenly
opened in her heart—a hole filled with soft, warm air.
She was floating in it. Her guilt and fear simply floated
away.

Then she forgot about thinking and just drifted. She

wanted to drift forever. _Just give up, Val. It's so easy._ Gilead's words echoed in her head hypnotically. Val felt as if she were poised on the edge of a diving board, twitching and scared, the wind blowing through her hair, the cool blue water inviting her.

She gulped for air. Then she took the leap. "Take me!" she cried.

twelve

Val was walking along the railway tracks that wove through downtown Kent, heading straight toward an oncoming train. Joel ran after her, yelling at the top of his lungs. She turned. Her jade eyes looked like glass buttons. She stared right through him.

"Val! Get off the tracks!"

He was almost close enough to lunge for the edge of her burgundy down jacket. Suddenly, a vacant smile curled on her lips and she stepped off the track and glided past him like a ghost, heading straight for the frigid, dark waters of the Cuyahoga River. Fingers of fear shimmied up Joel's spine.

He spun around and called after her again, waves of helplessness engulfing him. "Val, honey, come back! Don't leave me!"

Joel Bennigan bolted upright in his bed, sweat slicking his face and neck. *A nightmare. It's only a dream.* The only sounds were his labored breathing and the black rain slapping against his bedroom window. Then a freight train wailed.

He fell back on his dampened pillow, exhausted. *They've got her. I know they've got her. I should never have lost my temper. It's all my fault.*

He saw the lightning zigzag across the sky through his open mini-blinds. The sudden loud cracks of thunder seemed to kick him in the small of his back.

Joel turned over and punched his pillow. The loneliness was unbearable. Worse than the agony of wrecked knees. He squeezed his moist eyes shut and gave in to the pain of losing the most important person in his life. "Val," he whispered. "Val, I need you."

Snapping on his bedside light, Joel reached for his Bible. Flipping to the New Testament, he quickly found the verse that was dancing around the edge of his consciousness: "And you will know the truth, and the truth will make you free" (John 8:32).

Truth. Freedom. *That's Your promise, Lord. Only You can open her eyes to the truth and free her. I'm claiming this promise—for Val, and for me.*

When he'd yielded to his stupid anger and walked out on her three days ago, he'd lost her. He knew that. How could he expect any woman to put up with a temper like his? When she didn't show up at church on Sunday, he knew she'd gone to Michigan. The loss of her felt like a light had been switched off inside him, plunging him into darkness—a darkness from which he couldn't seem to emerge.

He couldn't go on like this. He had to get her back. Lord, help him. Then, like a flash of lightning, it hit him. He knew what he had to do. He prayed it wasn't too late.

≈

Joel wasn't dreaming this time. Val really was walking toward him. His heartbeat quickened. From his position on the wooded hillside, he watched her cross the grassy university Commons, handing cult literature to students on their way to class. She wore black slacks and her thick down jacket seemed to dwarf her.

"Charity!" he whispered urgently to his sister. "There she is! With a human watchdog."

Gilead trailed behind Val, also handing out pamphlets and collecting donations. Cult members always traveled in pairs, he recalled.

"At last," said Charity, kneading the knot out of her calf muscle. "It feels like we've walked every one of the eight hundred acres of this campus."

"You distract the guard, and I'll corner Val."

"Right," Charity said softly, touching Joel's forearm reassuringly. "Let's pray this works."

"It has to, Charity. I can't lose her."

In the four days since Val's return from Michigan, Joel had stopped by her apartment every morning. Tess had cried and told him Val was gone—she'd moved in with the Children of Last Days Light. "She acts like a different person," her distraught roommate had cried. "I've tried calling her, but they won't let me speak to her. Please, Joel, do something."

Do something. With a desperate prayer, Joel crossed the small brick plaza of the May Fourth Memorial tucked into the hillside. Meanwhile, Charity darted down the other side of the hill and approached Gilead from behind so Val wouldn't see her.

Joel positioned himself behind the four free-standing stone markers that reached for the sky in memory of the students slain by National Guardsmen during the anti-war demonstration on May 4, 1970. The bulky granite hid his large frame. He thought about the Vietnam War. He knew he was protesting a different kind of war—spiritual warfare for Val's soul. He'd launch his first offensive right here.

Between the balding trees he saw Charity talking to Gilead on the Commons. Even from the hill, he could see that his sister was putting on a convincing performance of enthusiastic interest in the pamphlets. Seconds later, Val trekked up the granite walkway toward the Memorial, glancing around as if she were looking for prospective buyers. But the hill was deserted. "Val!"

Startled, she spun around, dropping her stack of tracts.

"Oh, Joel. . .it's you," she said, her voice curiously flat. No emotion registered on her face, and she made no move toward him.

Instead, she bent to pick up the literature. In a moment, he was beside her, helping her retrieve the writings of Father Elijah from among the twigs and leaves.

"Oh, Joel, I'm so happy. I was so wrong about the Family. They're the most wonderful, loving, godly people I've ever met." Her tone sounded as if she were reciting a memorized speech. Her smile looked more like a grimace.

Joel's heart splintered as he looked at her. Her words said one thing, her body another. She looked haggard, pale, listless. What she *didn't* look was happy. Quickly, he picked up the remaining papers and, careful not to touch her, motioned her toward the stone bench facing the Memorial.

"I've been worried about you, Val. Why didn't you call me when you got back into town?" he asked as they sat down on the cold black marble.

"I—I. . ." She seemed at a loss for words. "Oh, I guess I was just too busy with the Lord's work. . . . New members have lots of studying to do. But I've wanted to ask you to stop by to meet the Family and attend a lecture. I don't think you've given them a fair hearing, Joel."

A fair hearing? Lord, give me patience.

"All's fair in love and war," he said.

"War?" Val stared at him blankly, almost as if she didn't see him. Her eyes looked vacant, like in his dream. He fought his desire to take her in his arms. He knew in his heart she wasn't his Val anymore. Sometime over the last week, she'd crossed an invisible line. She was one of the Children of Last Days Light now.

"War, Val. Do you know what this is?" He gestured toward the Memorial.

"No."

"The May Fourth Memorial. In the spring, the university plants 58,175 golden daffodils on this hill to symbolize each American lost in the Vietnam War. One is for your father. But you're a casualty, too."

Val's face fell.

"And I'm losing you to another war, Val—a spiritual one. You're a prisoner of war, held in Father Elijah's camp."

Her eyes narrowed. "What are you saying?"

This was his moment. She'd given him an opening.

"See these words on the Memorial, Val—*Inquire, Learn, Reflect?*" He pointed at the stone inscription. Her gaze followed.

"*Inquire,* Val." He grabbed her by the shoulders passionately. "*Learn, reflect* on what the cult has done to you—please! I'm begging!"

She shrugged out of his grasp. "They've given me peace, Joel—real peace. A way to make up for the failure I've been all my life. I'm with God's chosen ones now. With them, I can be good enough—maybe not for you—but for God."

She stood up and walked over to the cold slabs of dark pink granite. They looked like four giant tombstones marching over the rise of the hill, each one taller than the last. The pale sunlight gleamed off the polished surface as she ran her hand along the smooth stone.

"My father died in a worldly war." She pushed the words through stiff lips. "But I'm fighting for the truth."

Joel sighed. He wasn't getting through. "The truth is that they used your guilt about your mother to hook you, didn't they?" His mouth settled in a grim line.

She didn't answer. Instead, she studied the jagged pools of hazy golden light filtering through the trees.

He walked quietly to stand beside her. Then he hung back. The stiff set of her shoulders let him know she didn't want his touch. And after his temper tantrum in Brady's, he could hardly blame her.

But he had to keep trying to reach her. Already, he could feel her slipping away from him. "Val, these retreats are really choreographed. Even the spontaneous crying during testimonials is planned."

A muscle in her jaw twitched. She walked away quickly.

He followed, catching up with her. "They wear you down—then push you into an emotional crisis," he continued urgently, hoping that Charity could manage to keep the watchdog at bay a little longer. "The leaders weasel personal information out of you, then they use it against you. They asked about your mother, didn't they?"

Suddenly, she stopped and looked at him. A flicker of recognition crossed her face. Then she dropped her head and leaned, wearily, against the looming eight-foot marker, the largest of the four.

"Yes." Her voice was barely above a whisper.

Gently, he covered her trembling hand with his. "They're like therapists gone mad, honey. They induce a nervous breakdown. Then they tell you the only way out is to join them. It's barbaric."

He felt her tears fall on his hand. "Val?"

No reply. Her long auburn hair shrouded her face.

"Val, honey, don't you see—they're false prophets. We don't need to work for God's approval. Christ has already forgiven our sins.

"They've trashed God," Joel continued, his voice soft, drawing in his lips thoughtfully. "They've made Him into a tyrant instead of a loving Father."

When he heard a tiny sob, he reached for her and pulled her against him, hard. They were alone except for the black squirrels scurrying among the crackling brown leaves. The place smelled of rich, dark earth after the recent rains. Sweet quiet suffused them, separating them from the rest of the world.

"I'm sorry I got angry the other day and acted like an jerk," he whispered, trailing his finger around her chin. "It's no excuse—but I got mad because I was afraid for you. Because I love you."

Without warning, Val threw her arms around his neck, sinking her hands into his thick hair. She clung to him as if she were afraid he'd disappear. Only a few lone birds and her muffled sobs disturbed the stillness.

Joel shivered as he inhaled the warm, delicious smell of her. Only after she stopped sobbing and nestled closer did his lips slowly but hungrily trail across her cheek, tasting her tears, possessing her mouth.

When the lingering kiss ended, Val hid her face against his chest, and he tightened his arms around her protectively. She gave in to the flood of emotions that assailed her. *Confusion? Desire? Need?* Which one described what she was feeling for Joel Bennigan?

Then the emotion she'd taken care to bypass jumped to the forefront of her mind. *Love?* The word stabbed her like a sharp blade. *Absolutely not.* She couldn't risk loving someone who would surely reject her— who at this very moment was rejecting her because she'd found peace with the CLDL. She could never be what he wanted or deserved. He'd always be angry at her.

Her heart lurched as she wrestled with the meaning of what he'd said. He'd insisted she was wrong about the CLDL, totally wrong. But what about her experience in Michigan? It seemed so real. Even worse, he thought she was defective because she was the child of an alcoholic. Hadn't he said as much? Not good enough. Bad seed.

He'd hit a raw nerve—her rawest nerve. She stiffened. *Who does he think he is, telling me I'm wrong and weak? How dare he?* Fury, fueled by shame, rose in response to her vulnerability to him. She hardened her heart by erecting barriers of anger, as hard and real as the Memorial markers.

"Why are you telling me this stuff?" she snapped, suddenly disengaging from him and taking a backward step. Surprise, then disbelief flooded his face, as if she'd just doused him with a bucket of ice water. She could sense his mounting frustration. The cords in his neck stood out. His shoulders bunched.

"Val, you're in denial," he groaned in exasperation, clenching his teeth. "Can't you see that the Family has psychologically manipulated you? They'll use you to peddle Father Elijah's writings and build his empire.

"You're not working for God, Val. *This* stuff isn't the gospel of Christ!" he spat angrily, pointing to her stack of literature. As soon as the words were out of his mouth, he wanted to snatch them back. *Nice going, Bennigan. Drive her away with another temper tantrum.*

"Val—I'm sorry. . . ." Joel began. More frustrated than he could ever recall being in his life, he drove his fingers through his hair and struggled to regain control.

But Val had seen the anger flash in his eyes—then the coldness, as if the blue orbs had been chipped from a glacier. Immediately, she took his criticism as rejection. "Denial?" she echoed. "I'm not denying anything! You're denying the CLDL's true devotion to God's work!"

Her whole body tensed. Her head hurt. Despite her confident words, her thoughts tumbled in confusion. Joel's words triggered doubts within her. Last weekend, her decision had felt so right. She couldn't believe she'd made a horrendous mistake. That was too horrible to contemplate. Even the thought made her feel sick to her stomach

And even if Joel is right—how could he possibly love someone so gullible? He's already so angry with me. No, no, no. She couldn't believe she was wrong. She felt as if she'd climbed aboard a speeding train, and she couldn't risk jumping off. Not now.

She'd rather die than fail God. And if giving up Joel was the price of serving the Lord, well, so be it. She'd been warned. Moving as if in a trance, she pushed past him and headed toward the bench where she'd left her pamphlets. *God demands many sacrifices to prove our worthiness—just like Father Elijah said.*

"You're afraid to love me because you think I'll abandon you like your mother did, Val," Joel called after her, "but you're wrong. Dead wrong. You're making the worst mistake of your life," he pleaded, his empty hands outstretched.

"It's mine to make," she said, her voice a monotone. "I must forsake all. I advise you to do the same—before it's too late."

She turned her head and looked at him. A haunted look crept into her eyes. The color left her face.

"Don't leave me, Val," he begged, his voice barely above a whisper. Joel winced as he watched the shutter close over the window to her heart, helpless to stop it, and saw her tighten her jaw as she turned away from him.

Mechanically, Val picked up her literature, straightened the pile, and without another word, started briskly down the hill. She closed her eyes tight for a moment, only to see the agony on Joel's face again. She quickened her pace, her head high, tears flowing down her cheeks.

He didn't follow her. She knew he wouldn't. She could feel him, though, standing among the trees and monolithic markers. Alone. His eyes searing her back. She wanted to wipe the tears from her face, but she was too proud. He'd see the gesture.

This is for the best, Joel. You may think you love me, but you don't. You'll only leave me in the end.

Hauling in a shaky breath, Val ran the rest of the way down the hill, toward Gilead, who stood waiting on the edge of the Commons. Her heart thumped. She'd go where she was wanted. Where she could prove herself good enough.

She'd fling herself into the arms of the Family.

thirteen

"And your name shall be Tamar," Jeremiah announced solemnly.

Val sat, cross-legged, on the faded lime green carpet of the CLDL house. While everyone else was out selling tracts, Jeremiah had stayed behind to initiate her into the Family.

Already her belongings had been stashed away upstairs in the sisters' bedroom. Now, her new name signaled her acceptance into the group. She picked at the edges of her Bible nervously, avoiding Jeremiah's fiery gaze.

"Have you forsaken all, Tamar?" he pressed. "Possessions, car, bank accounts, loved ones? God wants *everything*. Remember, the early believers 'had all things in common.'

"Don't dare hold anything back from the Lord, sister, lest He destroy you like He destroyed Ananias and Sapphira," he said, his voice gravelly. "They withheld money from the apostles, you know."

Absolute commitment. Val squirmed. She had signed over her car, lugged her sewing machine, bicycle, household items, and clothes to the house for use by the brethren. Now she had the distinct feeling that wasn't enough.

"You don't mean my savings for college?" she asked

timidly.

"And what else would I be meaning?" he answered in his Irish brogue. "Trust God to provide your needs, little sister. What would you be wanting with an education anyway—with the end of the world so near? The real need is to help God's work, not to help ourselves."

Meekly, Val fetched her savings records, money she'd inherited after her mother had died. With trembling hands, she signed them over to Jeremiah. He smiled under his bushy black mustache and rewarded her with a bristly kiss on the cheek.

"Little sister Tamar, God is smiling down at you. This money will go a long way to spread the gospel in Ireland."

"Ireland?"

"Yes. I'll be leaving for Dublin on Saturday, and the Lord told me to take you along. We'll be joining Father Elijah's son, Shiloah, who's pioneering a center in Dublin."

Val's mind reeled, and she blinked. "Dublin? Ireland? You want me to leave the United States?"

"Oh, *I'm* not the one who's wanting it, Tamar," he said quickly, an edge of impatience in his voice. "'Tis the Lord who wants you to preach the gospel to the lost souls of the Emerald Isle."

He looked at Val's crestfallen face, cleared his throat, and continued, one beefy, black-haired hand resting piously on his Bible. "Our most important rule is obedience to leadership—immediate, absolute obedience without doubt or question. We are an army with military discipline. We follow the Bible: 'Obey them that have the rule over you, and submit yourselves: for they watch for your souls.'

"Doubts are the devil's thoughts, Tamar. You must chase them away. Blot them out with Bible verses or the Family chant. You must go to Ireland with me. God has spoken."

Val swallowed hard. "But—but what about my friends here in Kent?" she asked quietly, thinking of Tess and, more importantly, of Joel. How could she bear never to see him again?

"Friends? Don't you understand the meaning of 'forsaking all' yet?" He frowned and cocked his head. "Is it a special friend you're thinkin' of?"

Val's cheeks flooded crimson.

"Ah, I see." Jeremiah chuckled. "Who is he?"

"Joel Bennigan, assistant pastor of Faith Bible Church."

Jeremiah's face grew dark. "Sickening, lukewarm, churchy Christian!" he spat. "I've had a run-in with your hypocritical pastor. He's the one responsible for Kevin Milford leaving the Family and losing his soul."

Val remembered the night Joel had spoken with the boy from church. "He only wanted to help the kid," she said defensively.

"And send him to hell in the process!" Jeremiah stormed. "Don't you know what the Bible says about backsliders? God will smite those who turn back to the world." His voice rose to a thunderous roar. Val trembled.

"And you—little sister—are in danger of losing your

soul if you harbor feelings for this agent of the devil. Cut him out of your heart right now. Forget him. Forsake him and follow God! Obey the Bible and go into all the world to preach the gospel!"

છ

She had come only at Jeremiah's insistence. At least, that's what Val told herself as she paced back and forth in the waiting room outside Joel's office at the church. Jeremiah sat on the edge of the orange Naugahyde couch, arms crossed over his bulky chest. His frown impressed Val with the seriousness of their mission.

Cut yourself loose from the devil. His words rang in her head. *Burn all your bridges. Prove your faithfulness to God by kissing the enemy good-bye.* Of course, she was sure he hadn't meant a literal kiss. She was to shun Joel. Her loyalty to the Family—and her immortal soul—was at stake.

What did it matter if she formally broke her relationship with Joel? she asked herself again and again. She wasn't good enough for him anyway. He'd leave her, sooner or later. But at least she could prove her devotion to God's work by following Jeremiah's orders. After all, forsaking all was required by Christ for each and every disciple, including a new disciple named Tamar.

And to be sure she burned those bridges completely, Jeremiah had insisted on accompanying her for a face-to-face confrontation with Joel. "There's no turning back now," he warned in a throaty, patronizing voice when they reached the church. "Remember Lot's wife."

But Joel wasn't there, though the secretary had said he was due to return from the soup kitchen any minute. So they waited. But each minute felt like an eternity, and more than once, Val wanted to bolt.

Jeremiah's menacing expression stopped her. "Don't fail God now, Tamar."

Suddenly, the sound of masculine footsteps echoed on the wooden hall floor, and a shadow fell across the opaque glass door. Val drew in her breath sharply as the doorknob turned. Surprise flooded Joel's face the instant he saw her. "Val . . . ?"

Her mouth twisted in a jagged smile, unable to restrain a soft gasp that escaped when she saw the heartrending tenderness of his gaze. A tingling of excitement raced through her as she caught the beginnings of a smile of welcome on his lips. She had to fight her overwhelming need to throw herself into his arms.

He held out those arms and stepped toward her. But the sight of Jeremiah stopped him in his tracks. "*You!*" Joel spun around to face the bear-like man.

"Yes, it's me, Pastor Bennigan," Jeremiah said with disdain, rising to his full height. "And we've come to tell you that Tamar is through with you. As a servant of God, she wants no more fellowship with darkness."

"Tamar?" Joel's puzzled gaze fell on Val.

"The old Val has died, Bennigan. Tamar is a new creature in Christ, ready to spread God's light to the world."

Joel's face filled with horror. "Val, this can't be true! Tell me it's not so, my love. What have they done to you?"

"It's true, all right, Bennigan. Admit it—you've lost another one to the Lord." Jeremiah gloated unabashedly.

Joel seized Val by the shoulders. "Val, is this true? I need to hear it from you—not this bozo."

At his touch, shock waves coursed through her. Val closed her eyes and tried to calm her jumbled thoughts. This whole scene seemed so unreal. So much seemed unreal since she had come back from the retreat. She felt anchorless, like a small boat lost at sea with nothing to guide her. . .nothing except the words of Jeremiah after that mind-cracking session in Michigan: *Don't fail God again.*

She nodded, almost mechanically. "Jeremiah's right, Joel," she said softly, her voice strained and weak. "I've forsaken all to follow God—it's the Lord's will," she added in an effort to reassure herself as much as to convince him. But it didn't help. Her heart was breaking, and, from the crushed look on Joel's face, his was too.

"Val—you don't need to join a cult to serve God," Joel cried, his grip tightening on her shoulders. "Devoting yourself to Christ's service doesn't mean you have to follow Father Elijah. You look like you're in a trance. What did they do to you?"

Jeremiah moved closer. "The Scriptures say that if you're not with us, you're against us," he rumbled as he removed Joel's hands from Val.

Something snapped in Joel's brain then. The blood pounded in his temples, his hands began to sweat, and his breath grew labored. Old reactions took over. With a guttural roar, he threw off Jeremiah's beefy hand.

"Get out of my face, you liar!" he snapped savagely. "You know that's not what the Scriptures mean. You've browbeaten Val and duped her with mind manipulation and out-of-context Bible verses."

"Hey, hey, brother, don't get hot under the collar. This is the land of the free and I wouldn't force this American princess to do anything against her will. Would I, Tamar?" he baited her, spreading his hands in a mocking gesture of helplessness. But he also shot Val a warning glance.

She stood, transfixed by the raw tension between the two men. Even the air felt brittle with hostility.

"Val's her name," Joel said quietly, too quietly. Anger seethed in his eyes. "What else did you steal from her besides her name? Her money? Did you take her car? I know how you con-men operate."

"Sister Tamar has freely forsaken all," Jeremiah drawled. "Which is more than I can say for you, Bennigan, with your fancy house and rich daddy."

Joel turned to Val, his eyes imploring her for an answer. "Val?" On his lips, her name sounded like a gentle caress. "How could you do this to us? To yourself?"

Val saw tears forming in those sky-blue eyes. She took a deep breath before answering him. "It's true, Joel. I'm going to preach the gospel in Ireland," she said, hoping somehow that geographical distance would make the break more final.

She wanted to console him, but she knew there was nothing she could say to help him understand. Maybe he really was spiritually dead, as Jeremiah insisted.

"You're going *where?*"

"You heard her, Bennigan," Jeremiah interrupted gruffly. "The Lord's calling her to help pioneer the Family in pagan Ireland."

"More like you're taking her along to meet your own devious purposes," Joel growled, his eyes darkening and beads of perspiration sliding down his forehead.

That's when Val saw Joel's hand clench into a fist, rise, and suddenly smash into Jeremiah's face. Caught by surprise, Jeremiah reeled and slammed against the couch.

Joel jumped backward, as if he'd received an electric shock, and stood, aghast, looking at his fist as if it weren't attached to his arm. "Dear God. . .what have I done?" A glazed look of defeat spread across his features.

Val pressed her hand over her face as if to hide from the violence that had unfolded in front of her eyes. She felt a wretchedness of mind she'd never known before. A stab of guilt pierced her chest. Joel had lost his composure because of her. *I drove him to this.* Suddenly, she wanted to put as much distance as possible between herself and this man of God.

"See, I told you he was a hypocrite, Tamar," Jeremiah spat as he struggled to his feet, a thin thread of blood winding down his forehead into his eye. "I told you he was the agent of Satan. C'mon, sister, let's get out of here before he starts persecuting you for preaching the gospel too."

He grabbed Val by the arm and dragged her out of the waiting room. She looked back once and saw Joel standing in the middle of the room, stunned, staring at his fist in disbelief. As Jeremiah hustled her down the corridor, she thought she heard a choked cry of anguish.

⁂

Several minutes passed before Joel realized they had left. He let himself into his office, flung open the windows, and gulped in huge mouthfuls of cool, fresh air. Catching a glimpse of Val just before Jeremiah dragged her around the corner of Main Street, he yelled, "Val— beware of false prophets!" She didn't turn, and in two seconds, they had disappeared.

Joel sank down into his chair and buried his face in his hands. *Why did I have to lose my temper? I've driven her right into their arms. She'll think I'm rejecting her. Lord, what's wrong with me? Why can't I control this anger?*

He sat there for a long time, his tawny head resting on his desk. His heart ached like a lacerated wound. He'd violated his standards as a man of God. He'd further alienated the woman he loved. But was she still the same woman he'd fallen in love with? Val didn't even look like herself.

They'd even given her a new name! And what a name—*Tamar*—that unfortunate woman who'd made a brief appearance in the pages of Genesis. A woman violated and used by the men around her.

Joel shuddered. He hoped the new name wasn't prophetic.

fourteen

"Forget him, Tamar," Jeremiah ordered, his voice as dark and flinty as his eyes. "It's God's will that you break with Bennigan. 'Be ye not unequally yoked together with unbelievers.' Chase thoughts of him away with a Bible verse. It's Satan tempting you."

He glared at her across the large table strewn with Father Elijah's rambling writings. "You should be studying the truth, Tamar—not wasting the Lord's time moping after Joel Bennigan!"

Val swallowed hard and bit back her tears. The Family viewed weeping as weak and worldly, a lack of faith. To distract herself, she looked out the wide picture window at the magnificence of Dublin Bay.

Jeremiah's words brought her little comfort. Neither did the damp, cold Irish air that chilled her bones. Ever since they'd arrived in Dublin a week ago, the rain hadn't stopped. Neither had her thoughts of Joel Bennigan.

For one glorious, stolen moment, the beauty of the sea held her spellbound. Beyond the stark stones and black jagged rocks lay a brilliant jewel of silver-blue water that flowed peacefully toward the distant expanse of Irish horizon. If only she could feel so peaceful. In this moment, she'd almost forgotten Jeremiah. . . .

"Nice view, huh, Tamar?" he snarled, slamming the old wooden table with his fist. "But let's remember our mission and not get tripped off into sightseeing. God called us to warn the world of its wickedness, not to admire the view.

"When God's judgment comes down—as it will soon—the sea will turn red with the blood of innocent people condemned to hell because we didn't give them the message. Think about that, sister."

Val winced and forced herself to focus on the thick manual of Father Elijah's instructions for new disciples. But she couldn't concentrate. The Family's teachings revolved so much around God's wrath and retribution that she found herself living in a never-ending state of fear and anxiety. Her stomach was constantly upset. She was always on the verge of tears. She could never do enough to please God, never be good enough, never work hard enough. None of them could.

That guilt had driven her to throw herself totally into the cult's daily routine: rising before dawn, studying and listening to lectures until mid-morning, then distributing tracts and collecting money until dark. After several hours of chanting and singing back at the house, she would fall into a dreamless sleep on the floor in the unheated room she shared with the other sisters.

The November dampness permeated her life as much as Father Elijah's angry God. The Family lived in a drafty old house by the sea, the rent and utilities paid by local businessmen.

"I tell them we help young people with drug problems," Shiloah told the Family members privately. "Of course, we don't do it in the way *they* think we do. But that's the fault of their worldly, unspiritual minds. The flesh profits nothing. We help young people by giving them the message of Father Elijah."

Something about his logic bothered Val. She didn't think his representations to the business community were quite ethical. But since questioning a leader was unthinkable, she pushed her doubts to the back of her mind, where they languished on her mental scrap heap, along with her thoughts about Joel. Ever since that awful day at his office, she had tried to tell herself he was better off without her. He'd realize it sooner or later. Her mother had been right. She didn't deserve love.

Now, if she could only get to the point where she could stop thinking about him, longing for him, she'd be all right. Only no matter how long she chanted or how many Bible verses she repeated, she couldn't seem to get to that point.

Six months before Val and Jeremiah arrived, four CLDL leaders had moved to Dublin. Shiloah, a tall man with thinning brown hair caught back in a long ponytail, had been one of them. He, along with his meek wife, Martha, and another American couple, Ezekiel and Rebecca, had quickly attracted a core of Irish disciples.

Val tried hard to fit in with these other new disciples—Solomon, Joseph, Ezra, Jubilee, Bethel, and Rachel—but she found it next to impossible to make friends because all talk and activities revolved around the Family. Private conversations, as well as private thoughts, were forbidden. Another Family rule.

So she nursed her broken heart alone, in silence. But as she walked down Grafton Street with bubbly Jubilee, passing out Father Elijah tracts to young housewives pushing prams or disheveled street musicians playing tin whistles, she was picturing Joel's face the last time she had seen him. The pain that had flashed in his eyes when she announced she was leaving. The horror flooding his features after he'd slugged Jeremiah. A wave of guilt swept through her. She— and she alone—had caused it all. . . .

Work harder! .Sell more! Banishing thoughts of Joel, Val redoubled her efforts to spread the word. She turned herself into a human whirlwind, rushing from person to person, pushing literature into their hands and convincing them to donate to the Family.

ᴢ

"Rat-a-tat! Rat-a-tat!"

Shiloah burst into the living room, hollering at the top of his lungs and waving a toy machine gun wildly.

"Augh!" yelled Jeremiah, leaping to his feet. His arms shot up in surrender.

Gilead screamed. Jubilee burst into tears. Val gasped and felt her stomach knot into a hard ball of fear.

Menacingly, Shiloah panned the group of disciples sitting on the bare wooden floor with their books. Jeremiah had been expounding Father Elijah's prophecies about the last days.

The end has come, Val thought. *This is it, and I'm not ready.* She looked around at the panicked faces all around her. They must feel the same.

"Ha! How many of you guys were really prepared?" Shiloah taunted as he lowered the gun and strode to the center of the room, his long ponytail flying. The dim light emphasized the gauntness of his face. His pale green eyes glinted like hard stones. His high, sharp cheekbones and thin lips gave him a hungry, mean look.

Val caught her breath and realized this had been a warning, a preview of things to come, a foreshadowing of Father Elijah's prophecies. She cringed beneath Shiloah's scowl.

"It's going to happen, brothers and sisters—just that quickly." He snapped his fingers. "Don't forget that for one minute. We will be persecuted for our faith. We'll be captured, tortured, and even killed. But, if we're faithful, we'll stand with the Lamb. Hallelujah!"

Suddenly, Val felt a tickling in her nose. *Uh-oh! Not here, not now!* She tried to hold it back, but couldn't. A huge sneeze erupted and echoed around the bare room.

Shiloah spun around to find the source of the disruption. "Who. . .?"

Then Val succumbed to a coughing fit. Desperately, she tried to stifle the cough, but it persisted. She coughed, she wheezed, she sneezed. She'd never had a worse cold.

"What weak disciple doesn't have enough faith to

stay healthy?" Shiloah thundered.

All eyes fell on Val, red-nosed and still spluttering. Humiliated and embarrassed, she twisted her hands nervously in her lap. *If only I could disappear into the woodwork.* Another sneeze racked her body.

She glanced around pleadingly at her brothers and sisters seated cross-legged on the floor in a circle. Surely her cold had more to do with the damp, the unheated rooms, the fatigue, and the skimpy meals than with her spiritual weakness. But their hard, accusing stares told her she was at fault.

"Sister Tamar, we're going to pray that God will forgive you for your lack of faith and, in His mercy, restore you to health," Shiloah announced grimly, placing his bony hand on Val's head. "You're no good to God if you're sick. Do you *want* to be useless to God?"

Val shook her head and tried to stave off another cough. *If only I had some cough medicine. . .but it isn't allowed. All medicine is of the devil—it's a lack of faith.* Furtively, she wiped her nose.

Shiloah launched into a tirade. "Father Elijah has made it clear that sickness is sin!" he bellowed. "If you're sick, you're sinning. It's as simple as that. You're not trying hard enough to get the word out. You're harboring sinful thoughts in your heart, maybe thoughts of your life before you joined God's Family."

His eyes narrowed and his scornful gaze fell on Val. "Is your heart back in the world, sister?" he growled.

Val's heart raced. *Can he read my mind?* "Th—

there is someone I think about. . .sometimes. I try not to, though. . . ."

"I knew it! God would never afflict you if you weren't sinning," Shiloah crowed triumphantly. "Stealing time from God in your thoughts is the same as stealing the money you collect for Him on the streets."

Val bowed her head. She sniffled and struggled to breathe while Shiloah stood over her, shouting for God to forgive her backsliding heart.

Jeremiah led the rest of the group in chorusing "Amen," and soon the room was filled with a cacophony of loud prayers, wailing, and pleading with God.

Shiloah seemed to thrive on the electrifying atmosphere of fear as he bounded from person to person, shaking his accusing finger. "You—Brother Solomon—do you have sin in your heart? And what about you, Sister Jubilee? Have you truly forgotten your pagan husband? God breaks up worldly families at His whim to call His faithful ones to spread the word."

Jubilee's chin began to quiver. Tears splashed down her round, rosy cheeks.

"God will have no other gods before Him—even the god of marriage!" Shiloah shrieked.

While he ranted deep into the night, Val sat on the floor, trembling, her head bowed. Her body shook with chills and hot flashes. No one noticed.

When Shiloah dismissed them well after midnight, he ordered them to rise early to continue repenting. "God is purging our home of the faint-hearted," he said, glowering at Val. "And you—sister—you'd better get healed. And remember, God doesn't allow doctors or medicine."

❧

But Val's cold grew worse. She sniffled and shivered her way through the long, grueling days on the Dublin streets. Shiloah started calling her a "weak sister" because she didn't have the faith to get healed. Jubilee took pity on her and gave her an extra sweater, but nothing seemed to warm Val's chilled body and soul. Even in the early morning hours, the dampness crept into her sleeping bag.

Red bricks and gray fog. For Val, the ancient city—clothed in poetry—seemed to dissolve into a swirl of red bricks and gray fog as she pounded the streets, hour after hour, day after day. No matter how hard she tried, she couldn't stop hoping that she'd turn the corner of one of those streets and find Joel waiting for her. Or he'd bound out of some door and sweep her into his arms.

But he never did.

The rain usually began drizzling as the Family caught the cream double-decker bus after Shiloah's morning lecture. When they disembarked downtown on O'Connell Street, Shiloah paired them off. Often Val was teamed with Jubilee or sometimes with Jeremiah.

"Remember, brothers and sisters, we are God's last effort to save the world," he would remind them. "That's why we're called Children of *Last Days* Light. We're the last light before Judgment."

From the city's center, the teams fanned out on foot to win the Island of Saints and Scholars for Father Elijah. Trinity College, dating back to 1592, proved fertile ground for distributing tracts. As did St. Stephen's Green, a verdant gathering place in the heart of the city. Val found it easy to sell as many as three hundred pamphlets a day.

She and Jubilee often walked down the narrow, winding back streets, sometimes coming across open markets where old women in black shawls sold potatoes and produce from wooden handcarts. The old women accepted the tracts eagerly—although Val wondered if they'd be read—and often showed their gratitude with a gift of surplus vegetables.

Val's heart went out to the gypsy children, dressed in rags and dirty tartan blankets, begging on street corners. Often a child of ten or eleven would cradle an infant.

"Who are they? Where do they come from?" Val asked Jubilee one day.

"I've lived in Dublin all my life, and I'm still not sure," Jubilee replied. "Some say that centuries ago, around the time of the potato famine, people who were evicted from their farms took to the road."

"How tragic," murmured Val.

"Yes. . .but we have something in common with them," Jubilee said. Val had noticed Jubilee always kept her conversation centered around the Family, as was the rule. "We're also gypsies—for the Lord! We have no home, either."

Bitterness rose in Val's throat as she remembered

the Bennigans and how she had envied their close-knit family. How she'd wanted to be part of them. But that was a lifetime ago, part of her old, worldly life.

"We have no home," continued Jubilee, a quiver in her voice. "And, as soldiers of Christ, we have no family except each other."

Val noticed the woman's generous lower lip tremble. "You left your husband behind when you joined the Family, didn't you?" she probed, hoping to offer some comfort and perhaps open up a line of communication with Jubilee. Val craved real communication with another human being. Something personal. Something not centered on the Family.

Jubilee's mouth tightened. "Sister, you are out of the Spirit," she snapped. "My so-called husband rejected the word of the Lord, so it was God's will that I reject him. Shiloah told me so. We cannot allow our divine mission to be derailed by worldly love."

"Oh," said Val, feeling cut down to size by Jubilee's angry outburst. "Yes, of course. The Lord's work comes first."

"Don't you forget it, sister," Jubilee said. "I never think about that man. Those thoughts come from the pit of hell."

Val said no more, but something about Jubilee's denouncement of the covenant of marriage disturbed her. *'What God hath joined together, let no man put asunder'. . .but it seems Father Elijah can pull couples asunder at will. . . .*

"Are you talking to the devil?" Jubilee interrupted

Val's thoughts.

"Of course not." Val tried to look busy tidying her stack of pamphlets.

"Good, I'd hate to have to report you to Jeremiah and Shiloah. Now, let's get God's message out."

But no matter how hard Val tried to distract herself by peddling tracts, her thoughts always returned to Joel. She wished he could share Dublin with her— the mystery of the gypsies, the glory of Trinity, the charm of the literary quotes on public buildings. But that was not to be. Joel was her past; the Children of Last Days Light, her future.

Joel Bennigan wasn't the only unwelcome intrusion Val tried to ignore. Hunger pangs also plagued her. Despite the large amounts of money they collected, the group subsisted on donated wilted vegetables and stale bread. But since physical concerns were unspiritual, Val never complained about her hunger or her cold. That's why Jeremiah's sudden concern over her health came as such a surprise. . . .

The day had started out badly. Val had awakened aching all over, unable to stomach the breakfast of watery oatmeal. Her heart sank when Shiloah paired her with Jeremiah. Working with him was usually an exercise in oppression.

But Jeremiah acted differently that day. Val's selling went poorly. At four o'clock, Jeremiah suggested they stop for afternoon tea. "You look so tired and hungry," he said.

Val couldn't believe her ears. She felt thoroughly dumbfounded when he awkwardly put his heavy arm around her shoulders and guided her into Bewley's coffee shop on Grafton Street.

After a snack of pork pies and strong black tea, Val felt refreshed, but Jeremiah's behavior still puzzled her.

"I've been praying for you, Tamar," he said, pouring her a second cup of tea. "God is testing your faith with this cold."

When he smiled, Val couldn't help thinking that on his hardened face, a smile looked more like a grimace. "I hope so," she said meekly.

"Tamar, I've something to tell you. I mean. . .the Lord has shown me something. . .something you need to know."

Val's curiosity was aroused.

"I was praying and the Lord told me. . . ."

"Yes?" she probed. "What did the Lord tell you?"

"I was praying for a wife," he said with a twisted smile, "and the Lord just said, 'Why don't you marry Tamar?'"

fifteen

"M—Marry. . .*you and me?*" The words stuck in Val's throat. She didn't move a finger or blink an eyelid. The thought paralyzed her, and she felt ill.

"Yes, Tamar. God showed me it's His will." Jeremiah caught her hand in his sweaty, meaty grip.

Val tried to pull away, but his grip only tightened. Desperately, she struggled to find something to say, anything. The bustle of the room, the clanging of silverware and the chatter of the afternoon tea drinkers grated on her nerves unbearably. She felt trapped. "The Lord hasn't shown me anything about marriage to you," she sputtered finally. *Surely Jeremiah will respect an appeal to a higher authority.*

"He will, Tamar. He will. Just wait and see."

Val swallowed nervously and silently prayed that this was all a mistake.

In the days that followed, Jeremiah was attentive, even kind. Val found it more and more difficult to deflect his attempts at courtship, especially since Shiloah had announced that the marriage was most definitely God's will. God had shown him in a dream, Shiloah insisted—a pronouncement that almost frightened Val out of her wits.

❧

He'd been watching her for three days now and knew

her routine. Around mid-morning, Val and her partner—often a small, rotund woman with rosy cheeks—
walked around the lake in St. Steven's Green, distributing tracts to people out for an afternoon stroll or
relaxing on one of the many park benches.

But sometimes that hairy ape accompanied her, always trying to drape his huge arm over her thin shoulders. From his hiding place behind the bushes and
trees, he could make out the disgust on her face. Somehow, so far, she had managed to shrug off the ape's
advances.

As he watched, he found himself clenching his fists,
almost involuntarily. *No. No. By now I should have
learned that there's a better way.*

How tired and bedraggled she looked! Just seeing
her like this tore his heart open. She moved as if she
were walking in a fog. She probably was. Father
Elijah's fog of delusion, twisted half-truths, and out-
right lies. *Not for much longer, my love. Not if it
takes my last breath,* he vowed.

At the north end of the lake, the huge chestnut trees
could hide Val from her partner's view, at least temporarily—just long enough for him to carry out the
second stage of his plan. But the time had to be right.
Timing was everything in this war. His ducks weren't
lined up, not yet. But when they were, *boom!* He'd
blow Father Elijah and his crew of con-men right out
of the water—without resorting to physical violence
this time.

For now, though, all he could do was watch. Watch
and pray. She looked so thin—she must have lost ten

pounds since she'd walked out of his office and his life. She always seemed sick, shivering despite her down jacket, nursing one whopper of a cold. He often spied her sneaking a moment's rest on a bench. *I've got to get to her in time. Dear Lord, help me find the ammunition I need.*

∎

"You must be Reverend Bennigan," said the short Irish matron, extending her plump arm to shake his hand. "Come in, laddie. Ye must be fairly perishin' with the cold. I'll warm ye up a drop of tea."

"Hot tea would be nice, Mrs. MacGuire." Joel stepped inside the comfortable Dublin home of this affable woman and her husband, a deacon in a nearby church.

"This is me husband, Jack." The woman motioned toward a heavy-boned man with a mop of reddish hair. "And my name is Birdie."

"Our colleagues in America told us you'd be coming," Mr. MacGuire said as he took Joel's jacket. "The Anti-Cult Network practically spans the world, ye know. But 'tis unfortunate that we're needed."

"Well, I'm grateful that people like you are helping fight the cults," Joel said, accepting a delicate china cup of steaming, fragrant Earl Grey tea.

"Do sit down, Reverend. Would ye like a scone? With butter?" Mrs. MacGuire passed Joel a plate of warm, fluffy, round biscuits.

Joel found them denser and sweeter than American biscuits, but delicious nevertheless.

"More tea, Reverend?"

Joel chuckled. "I've drunk more tea in the last three days than in all my previous life! If I drink any more, I'm afraid I'll float away!"

"Ah, yes," sighed Mr. MacGuire. "Frequent tea drinking is our national vice, I'm afraid. But I'm sure ye'll get used to it. Now, tell us your story, son. You laugh, but I see pain in your eyes."

Joel drew a deep breath and let the story tumble out. His love for Val. Her class research project that had gone awry. Her entrapment into the CLDL. His violent attempt to stop her.

"I'm ashamed of my reaction," he admitted. "My temper is something I've struggled with ever since I came to Christ. My thorn in the flesh, perhaps."

"I understand, son," Mr. MacGuire said, resting a brawny hand on Joel's shoulder. "God lets us struggle with these weaknesses to keep us humble and dependent on His grace."

Joel nodded solemnly, comforted by the understanding he saw in the older man's face.

"In the tissue of mystery that is our lives, God's road map alone is infallible and steers us out of the danger zones to our souls," Mr. MacGuire continued. "So His word admonishes us to 'be angry, but sin not.' In other words, be angry for a just cause—but don't let that anger degenerate into hatred.

"God is pure love. Satan is pure hatred," he added, his steady gaze focused on Joel. "That's where we must be careful concerning the cults. We must hate the sin but love the sinner."

Joel nodded again.

"And to do that, we must fight with the sword of truth, not our fists."

"Amen!" Joel cried. "Mr. MacGuire, you must make a fine preacher."

"I try, son. But as far as the sword of truth—that's where our Barry comes in. He's our oldest boy, a journalist with *The Irish Times*. And when our Ann was nearly lured into the Family four months ago—would you believe they tried to recruit her right outside her high school?—Barry moved heaven and earth to investigate the group."

"What did he find?"

Mr. MacGuire shook his head. "It's unbelievable, absolutely unbelievable what they get away with in the name of religion. For a start, Jeremiah—who's originally from Dublin—has a prison record a mile long."

Joel gasped and set his cup down on the mahogany end table. That ape who'd tried to cozy up to his Val! He forced himself to stay calm and breathe deeply. "This isn't good news, Mr. MacGuire. Jeremiah recruited Val into the cult."

"Yes. They sent him to the States to act as a liaison between the IRA and the American gunrunners."

Joel's head began to spin. *Gunrunners? The Irish Republican Army? Terrorism? Val?*

"Jeremiah's legal name is Garret Foley. He started out as a petty thief—breaking and entering, bad checks, purse-snatching—that type of thing. Then he advanced to blackmail and gunrunning to the North. We strongly suspect he funnels cult money to the IRA.

We've only to catch him in the act."

Joel didn't want to hear any more, but he knew he needed to, for Val's sake. "This is how they use the money Val and the others collect for Father Elijah?"

"Exactly. And the CLDL brings in a fantastic amount of tax-free dollars all over the world—millions of dollars a year, especially in the United States," Mr. MacGuire answered. "They support other terrorists also, principally in the Middle East.

"And, of course, the top leaders live in luxury—huge houses, fancy cars, big swimming pools," supplied Joel angrily, filling in with his own knowledge of the subject. "But the lowly disciples like Val are kept hungry, deprived, and sick so they don't have the energy to wonder where the money is going."

The only sound in the room came from the crackling fire in the carved mahogany fireplace.

"I can't believe it—I don't *want* to believe it," Joel cried after a few moments. He buried his face in his hands. For a stunned second, he couldn't breathe. "Why? Why support terrorism and the killing and bombing of innocent men, women, and children? It doesn't make any sense."

"Father Elijah's secret writings—which Val won't be allowed to see for years—instruct the group to support terrorism." Mr. MacGuire sighed heavily and glanced over at his wife who sat at the edge of the chintz couch, wringing her lace-edged handkerchief.

"They believe that by promoting mayhem, they'll hasten the end of the world," he said, his deep voice tinged with incredulity. "The sooner society falls, the sooner the CLDL will be snatched away into heaven. They also believe they'll return to rule the earth during the millennium."

"What?" Joel's head shot up like a bullet from a gun. "Promoting terrorism for their own selfish gain?"

"Yes. They say they do evil that good may come," Mr. MacGuire said sadly. "In complete contrast to the loving, forgiving God that Jesus taught. But, as you know from your studies of cults, the end always justifies the means," he continued. "Ethical standards and objective truths are all bent to serve the purposes of the group."

"What are we going to do?" Joel asked softly, his voice a pain-filled whisper.

"How much danger are you willing to put yourself in, son?"

"For the woman I love—whatever it takes."

Mr. MacGuire smiled. "I didn't expect any less of you, young man. This is the plan. Tomorrow, you and Barry will trail Shiloah and Jeremiah after the rest of the Family disperses downtown. Our sources tell us they may be meeting this man—" He handed Joel a black and white mug shot.

"This character, Finn O'Dywer, is a known terrorist and an old friend of Foley's. We need evidence of a money exchange between them."

Joel nodded dumbly. The revelation had hurt more than if someone had slammed a fist into his stomach.

"Jack and I can't trail them because Foley would recognize us from our TV interviews on the cult," Mrs. MacGuire interjected. "Why, we've even had death threats over the telephone. Our tires have been slashed. And two weeks ago, a brick came flyin' through our window."

"It was a warning," her husband added. "The InterPol in Europe are investigating several suspicious deaths of people who criticized the CLDL."

"We've called our police—the Garda—but they say they need more evidence before they can give us protection," Mrs. MacGuire added with a worried frown.

"So we're on our own," said Mr. MacGuire, exchanging a determined look with his wife.

Joel shook his head, gazed blankly at the carpet. "May God help and protect us," he murmured. He raised his head and looked Jack MacGuire straight in the eyes. "Val has got to come with us tomorrow."

sixteen

"Val! Val! Over here!" A disembodied baritone rumbled from the darkness behind the trees.

Val stopped stock still in a dusky patch of light beside the neatly trimmed rows of bushes. She scanned the wooded area edging the north side of St. Steven's Green lake.

What was that? She listened again. But the only sounds she could hear were the whistles and honks of city traffic and the water lapping the edge of the pond. Overhead, a few wild geese cried. *My imagination's working overtime.*

Then the voice came again, soft as the wind whispering through the leaves. "Val! Over here!"

There was something familiar about that voice. The voice that haunted her dreams. Only, it couldn't be. . . .

She spun around to see if Jubilee was calling, but her partner stood quite a distance away, deeply engrossed in an intense debate with a young biker. Hesitantly, her heart pounding, Val stepped off the path that meandered around the lake, and picked her way among the massive chestnut trees.

Just then Joel stepped out from behind a tree trunk.

She gasped, her hand flying to her mouth. *"You!* How. . .when. . .?"

The sight of him stunned her like an electric shock. His jeans and snug-fitting jacket emphasized his angular, bold build. A strand of tawny hair had fallen across his broad forehead, and there was something about his stance, some hint of tightly leashed power, that struck a responsive chord deep within her soul.

Then her gaze fell on his gleaming cream-and-gray snakeskin cowboy boots. Quiet a contrast to the sneakers and loafers she remembered him wearing back in the States. Suddenly, the boots stuck her as outlandish. In spite of her shock, she laughed.

A smile spread across his face. "The Irish expect us Yanks to look like cowboys, and I didn't want to disappoint them," Joel drawled. "These boots are very comfortable, actually, for tromping through Dublin and around Steven's Green—trailing the woman I love."

He came for me. Val blinked and swallowed hard.

He moved toward her slowly, tentatively. "I need to know one thing, Val," he began, his voice suddenly low and serious. "Do you still love me?" He whispered the words in a husky, almost pained voice and stretched out his arms in a pleading gesture. Val could see longing in his clear blue eyes. Those eyes, that face, those arms she couldn't forget. *Do I still love him?* Did she still breathe? Did her heart still beat?

"Yes," she replied in a small voice. Tears filled her eyes as she lowered her gaze. *Does he still love me? Truly? After the way I've hurt him?*

The twigs and leaves crackled beneath Joel's booted feet as he stepped nearer. She looked up and saw him grin as he gathered her into his embrace. His kiss felt soft and gentle, and she felt his tenderness, treating her as if she were as delicate as fine porcelain. The kiss deepened as his hands roamed over the back of her jacket, arching her closer, seeking to fuse them together for all eternity.

When it ended, he held her close, his chin resting on the crown of her head. "It's time to go home, baby," he said, at last. "The Irish don't celebrate Thanksgiving."

Reluctantly, inhaling the comforting, familiar smell of him, Val stiffened and stepped away. He tried to pull her into his arms again, but she shook him off.

"I can't go back with you. I'm here on a mission for God."

"Honey, it's not God you're serving," he corrected her gently. "And I can prove it. I have evidence." He moved closer, but stopped when she edged away.

She backed up against a wide tree trunk until she was touching the rough bark. Taking a deep breath as if she were struggling to maintain her composure, she asked, "Evidence? What evidence?"

"Proof that the CLDL are nothing but a bunch of terrorist, gunrunning thugs." Joel chose his words deliberately, hoping to shock her back into thinking for herself again.

What little color there was in Val's sick, pale face drained away. "That's not true! It can't be. We serve God!"

"I'm sorry, my love, but I can prove my allegations," Joel said slowly, as kindly as he could.

She shook her head violently. "You're mistaken about the Family, Joel. You always have been!"

Cautiously, he held out his hand toward her. "Come with me and I'll show you the truth."

She closed her eyes and shook her head again. "No. It's a lie. Our enemies spread lies about us."

Joel waited a few seconds. When he spoke, his voice was warm. "Val, ever since I met you, I've admired your dedication to truth. That dedication makes you a fine journalist and an honest person." He could see tears steal out from beneath her closed eyelids.

"Let's make a wager, Val, just like Pascal," he continued. "If you're right, you've got nothing to fear. But if you're wrong, you've got to get out of the Family—fast."

Val shook her head again, still refusing to open her eyes.

"You owe it to yourself to find out the truth, Val. You owe it to yourself as a journalist, as a daughter of God, as the woman I love, and as one who—I believe—still loves me too. . . ."

Val's eyes sprang open. She blinked, then focused her gaze on Joel. He saw a flicker of vulnerability in those tired jade eyes before she looked away and stared dully at the ground.

He reached into his knapsack and pulled out the package Jack MacGuire had prepared for him—his front line ammunition. First, he handed Val the mug shot. "This, my love, is Finn O'Dywer, an IRA gunrunner."

Val recovered a little. "What's he got to do with the

Family?" she asked defensively.

"Plenty, I'm afraid. Take a look at this." He handed her Jeremiah's prison record. "Recognize the face? His real name is Garret Foley. The 'man of God' has a record a mile long. Robbery, battery, blackmail, gunrunning. Plus he's a long-time buddy of O'Dywer."

Shock, then disbelief crossed Val's face. "What are you saying?" she asked in a tremulous whisper.

"The money you and the others collect by the sweat of your brow—the money donors believe goes to drug addicts—is used by Jeremiah—I mean Garret Foley—and O'Dywer to fund the IRA," Joel said matter-of-factly, his brow furrowing. He felt the old anger beginning to rise, but held it in check.

"That can't be true!" With a moan of distress, she looked at him pleadingly.

"I wouldn't lie to you, Val," he said softly. "Come with me. We'll see if it's true or not."

"No. I won't go."

"Val, if you won't believe me—believe Father Elijah." *Dear Lord, this has got to work. This is my last bullet.*

Joel handed her a small stack of secret letters from Father Elijah. "You wouldn't be allowed to read these for several more years," he said quietly. "These are Father Elijah's instructions to support and fund terrorist organizations around the world."

"Oh!" Val's eyes misted over and she felt as if she couldn't breathe. With trembling hands, she took the letters and examined them. They appeared to be genuine—Father Elijah's familiar style, the same inane cartoons, the same cluttered typeset. But she hadn't heard this message before.

"The money goes to terrorists, my love. There are no drug programs."

Val noticed that Joel's voice suddenly sounded a million miles away, but she strained to hear as he went on. "They teach you to say that the money goes for drug rehabilitation programs, don't they?" he probed.

Val nodded dumbly, a tear stealing down her cheek. She'd always had a bad feeling about that line. Why hadn't she listened to her doubts? Suddenly, she felt nauseated. She slouched against the tree and slid down to the damp, mossy ground, clutching the papers.

Joel hunkered down beside her, his broad frame sheltering her from the cold wind that had sprung up. "Come with me, Val. Together we'll discover the truth about the CLDL," he said gently, taking her cold hand. "Jeremiah may meet with Foley today. Let's find out the truth—and let the truth set us free."

Val looked up at him, her eyes filled with tears. She said nothing. She couldn't.

"Do you trust me, Val?"

For a long moment, she couldn't force the words out. Then, ever so softly, she whispered, "I think so."

"Good, that's a start."

છ

Joel saw Barry's hands tremble on the wheel as he maneuvered in the heavy stream of lunch-time traffic pouring down O'Connell Street. The wet, slick streets left by the morning downpour did nothing to calm either man's nerves.

"Don't lose them," Joel urged.

"Don't worry," answered the young reporter, his hawk-like eyes tracking Jeremiah and Shiloah as the pair dodged and weaved among the crowds milling along the broad sidewalks.

Joel, Barry, and a silent Val shadowed the leaders as they crossed the angry-looking waters of the Liffey and wound down the narrow, cobbled side streets flanking the river. Shiloah carried a small black satchel on his shoulder.

"The crowds are thinning out here," Joel observed.

"Right. This part of Dublin is off the beaten path for the shoppers and business people," replied Barry, who looked like a younger version of his father.

"Are you all right, Val?" Joel squeezed her hand briefly. She nodded miserably, and Joel forced himself to resist putting his arm around her, even though the back seat was so cramped that they sat shoulder to shoulder.

They drove past several tall, boarded-up old buildings, covered with graffiti. A desolate, sooty feeling pervaded the deserted streets. The word *seedy* sprang to Joel's mind. An occasional double-decker bus screamed around the sharp corners, startling them as Barry grimly hugged the left curb with his Fiat. *Good thing the cars are small in Ireland,* Joel thought.

"Any ideas where they're headed?" he asked Barry.

"My guess would be the establishment straight ahead." Barry's nod indicated a small pub on Poolbeg Street. "This place has a reputation for being a watering hole for unsavory types."

"Huh. Maybe we'll hit pay dirt today."

"God willing."

Val said nothing. She was devouring the sandwiches and coffee Joel had brought along for her.

After Barry parked the car a safe distance from the public house, he and Joel hid behind opened copies of *The Irish Times*. Val slid down on the seat so as not to be seen.

Jeremiah and Shiloah disappeared into the dark, smoky cavern beyond the glossy black door. A sign outside boldly proclaiming "Guinness Is Good for You!" showed a pint of black brew with a thick, creamy head. Even at noon, rough-looking tradesmen and the unemployed were hard at work lifting pints.

Joel raised an eyebrow. "So early?"

"Well, yes. They've got to get some drinking in before the pubs close for Holy Hour from three to four in the afternoon," Barry explained.

"*Holy Hour?*" Joel exclaimed.

Barry let out a heavy sigh. "It's the law in Dublin. It might be the only time these men go home during the day to see their wives and children. May God be merciful. Drink can be a dreadful curse."

"Don't I know?" Joel shook his head, thinking of himself in bygone years, and, to his surprise, of Val's mother.

"But alcoholism is useful to the CLDL," continued Barry. "If the disease is in a person's family, you can be sure the cult recruiters will use it to their own advantage during the brainwashing process."

Joel shot Val a discreet glance. She'd finished her

sandwich and was looking out the window. He couldn't see her face.

"They use sensitive personal information as a kind of emotional blackmail. . . . Oh, look there—" Barry interrupted himself to motion toward a muscular little man with black curly hair, riding down the street on an old bicycle. He looked like a body builder, Joel noted.

"It's him!" Barry cried excitedly, jabbing at the photograph of Finn O'Dwyer. "I knew it. A money exchange. Our boy-o's have just done themselves in."

Beside him, Joel felt Val's body stiffen.

The man, whom Joel guessed to be in his late thirties, leaned his bike beside the beveled square window of the pub, glanced around, and strode jauntily inside.

"Thank God!" Barry breathed, turning to Joel, his hazel eyes twinkling and his ruddy face flushed more than usual. "Now all we have to do is wait."

Twenty minutes later, the three men emerged, smoking cigarettes and laughing. Much back-clapping and hand-shaking ensued. The scene looked like a reunion of old classmates.

"Can you get a photo?" Joel whispered from behind his newspaper.

"Yeah, they haven't even glanced this way. They're probably so happy on the goodness of Guinness, they've let down their guard."

Click! Another back slap for Jeremiah.

Click! Shiloah handed the black bag to Finn O'Dwyer.

Click! O'Dywer admired a wad of bills.

Click! Jeremiah shook the terrorist's hand.

Click! Click! The IRA man pedaled away. Shiloah and Jeremiah ambled back into the pub, puffing and laughing.

"I guess they're not going to save many souls today," Joel said grimly, his lips thinning.

"Nah, too busy celebrating the end of the world," Barry observed dryly. "C'mon, let's get the evidence developed. I can do it in an hour back at the paper's darkroom."

Throughout the entire exchange, Val sat silent and ashen-faced.

❧

"I can't believe it," she cried, beginning to sob as soon as Barry left her alone with Joel. Sitting in the parked Fiat along a Dublin side street, they waited while Barry ran to develop the photographs. "I gave up everything . . .even you! I really believed I was doing God's will . . . ."

She looked up at Joel. The anguish in her tear-filled eyes almost broke his heart. "Believe it, my love. Only the truth will set you free," he said, his voice velvet-edged and strong. "And it's also true that I love you and always will, no matter what."

His last words were her undoing. A loud sob escaped Val as Joel gently took her in his arms. To Val, those arms felt strong and safe, a haven from the pain that squeezed her heart unmercifully. *How could I have been such a fool? How could I ever have left this man for a farce?* Deep sobs racked her body, and she let out a low, tortured cry.

"It's OK to cry, Val," Joel soothed as she yielded to the compulsive sobs that shook her. Gently, he ran his hand through her hair. "Lean on me for now. We'll get through this together. It's *our* problem. You're not the first one they've duped—and, unfortunately, you won't be the last."

She fell against him with a moan. Yes, she'd made a mess of things, but with Joel by her side, she could face anything, do anything to give their love a second chance. Including tearing herself away from the Family and their pernicious hold on her.

Joel's love would give her the strength. The truth would show her the way. As she felt the warmth of his arms wound tightly around her, she knew she was where she belonged—where she'd always belonged. She'd come home. She wasn't alone anymore.

🙠

Val peered out the airplane window as the Emerald Isle shrank into a tiny green dot. So many big things had happened to her on that small island, she thought wistfully. With Joel's help, she had found the courage to leave the Family forever. She had written an article exposing the cult. And today she was on her way to freedom—back to the States with the man she loved.

Absentmindedly, she fingered the newspaper clip of her story, the story that had started an official governmental investigation of the CLDL in Ireland. The story that had served to break through Jubilee's defenses and caused her to leave the Family and return to her husband. Val couldn't wait to hear what Weston had to say about her work.

"It's the best thing I've ever read about a cult experience," Joel had said when the story had appeared in *The Irish Times* two days earlier. "It's a fantastic piece of investigative journalism. Weston will be impressed."

When the clouds finally blocked her view, Val fell back into her seat, leaning against the headrest. "Those are probably rain clouds," she said with a sigh, shooting Joel an exasperated smile. "I don't care if I never feel another raindrop in my life."

He chuckled, his eyes full of tenderness. His gaze rested on her face, as soft as a caress. Then his hand came down over hers possessively as he reached over to place a gentle kiss on her cheek. "By the way, I've got a surprise for you from the land of damp, rainy mists."

"Oh?" Val was curious.

She carefully put the newspaper clip back in her purse and with trembling hands opened the small, black velvet box Joel offered shyly. Inside lay a gleaming gold band formed in the shape of two hands encircling a heart. On top of the heart rested a crown.

"It's called a Claddagh ring," Joel explained. "It's an ancient Irish love symbol that originated in a small fishing village in the west of Ireland, near Galway."

Val ran her finger over the smooth gold. "It's beautiful, Joel. I've never seen anything like it."

"Traditional folklore has it that if you wear the heart facing outward, you're single. But if the heart points inward—toward your heart—you're spoken for."

Val smiled as Joel took the ring out of the box and slipped it on her ring finger, the heart facing inward. Her own heart sang with delight and she felt a warm glow spread through her body.

"Yes, I'm spoken for," she said softly.

"Have I told you that I love you?" He traced her chin lovingly with his forefinger.

"Only a few thousand times. But don't let that stop you."

"sAnd do you believe me? With all your heart?"

Val reached out and touched his face with a steady hand. "With all my heart. I believe I'm loved just as I am—by you and by God. I'm beginning to realize just how much my insecurities about my childhood had left me vulnerable to the cult's manipulation." She shook her head sadly.

"Joel," she said, gazing at him intently, "when we get back, will you come with me to the Adult Children of Alcoholic meetings in the church? I want to understand more."

"There's nothing I'd like more, my love. Nothing. We'll learn together."

"Yes. Together," Val said, nestling into Joel's comfortable shoulder, peace covering her like a warm blanket.

"Joel," she murmured sleepily, "I think I finally understand what Paul was saying in his epistles. We don't have to earn love. We don't have to be good enough for love." She smiled up at him. "Love is God's tender gift."

A Letter To Our Readers

Dear Reader:

In order that we might better contribute to your reading enjoyment, we would appreciate your taking a few minutes to respond to the following questions. When completed, please return to the following:

Rebecca Germany, Editor
Heartsong Presents
P.O. Box 719
Uhrichsville, Ohio 44683

1. Did you enjoy reading *Love's Tender Gift*?
   ❏ Very much. I would like to see more books by this author!
   ❏ Moderately
      I would have enjoyed it more if _____

   _____

2. Are you a member of *Heartsong Presents*? Yes   No
   If no, where did you purchase this book? _____

   _____

3. What influenced your decision to purchase this book? (Check those that apply.)

   ❏ Cover   ❏ Back cover copy
   ❏ Title   ❏ Friends
   ❏ Publicity   ❏ Other _____

4. On a scale from 1 (poor) to 10 (superior), please rate the following elements.

___Heroine ___Plot

___Hero ___Inspirational theme

___Setting ___Secondary characters

5. What settings would you like to see covered in *Heartsong Presents* books?

_____

_____

6. What are some inspirational themes you would like to see treated in future books?_____

_____

_____

7. Would you be interested in reading other *Heartsong Presents* titles? ❑ Yes ❑ No

8. Please check your age range:
❑ Under 18 ❑ 18-24 ❑ 25-34
❑ 35-45 ❑ 46-55 ❑ Over 55

9. How many hours per week do you read? _____

Name _____

Occupation _____

Address _____

City _____ State_____ Zip _____

Classic Fiction for a New Generation

Pollyanna
and
Pollyanna Grows Up

*Eleanor H. Porter's classic stories of an extraordinary
girl who saw the good in everyone. . . and made
everyone feel good about themselves.*

___*Pollyanna*— An orphan dutifully taken in by her repressive
aunt, the well-heeled Miss Polly Harrington, Pollyanna Whittier
reinvents a game of her father's and finds a way to hide her tears.
No one can resist Pollyanna for long and soon almost everyone
is playing "the Glad Game," everyone except Aunt Polly.
BTP-65 $2.97

___*Pollyanna Grows Up*—Ruth Carew's refined Boston world
has just been turned upside down. The reason, of course, is
obvious: Pollyanna Whittier has come to visit. From Boston to
Beldingsville to Europe and back again, *Pollyanna Grows Up*
continues the adventures of an irrepressible American girl on the
brink of womanhood at the turn of the century. In everything she
does—especially the Glad Game—Pollyanna reflects the bound-
less love of her Heavenly Father. BTP-80 $2.97

Send to: Heartsong Presents Reader's Service
P.O. Box 719
Uhrichsville, Ohio 44683

Please send me the items checked above. I am enclosing
$_____(please add $1.00 to cover postage and handling
per order. OH add 6.5% tax. PA and NJ add 6% tax.).
Send check or money order, no cash or C.O.D.s, please.
To place a credit card order, call 1-800-847-8270.

NAME _____

ADDRESS _____

CITY/STATE _____ ZIP _____

POLLY

Heart♥ong

Any 12 Heartsong Presents titles for only $26.95 *

CONTEMPORARY ROMANCE IS CHEAPER BY THE DOZEN!

Buy any assortment of twelve *Heartsong Presents* titles and save 25% off of the already discounted price of $2.95 each!

*plus $1.00 shipping and handling per order and sales tax where applicable.

HEARTSONG PRESENTS TITLES AVAILABLE NOW:

__HP 3 RESTORE THE JOY, *Sara Mitchell*
__HP 4 REFLECTIONS OF THE HEART, *Sally Laity**
__HP 5 THIS TREMBLING CUP, *Marlene Chase*
__HP 6 THE OTHER SIDE OF SILENCE, *Marlene Chase*
__HP 9 HEARTSTRINGS, *Irene B. Brand**
__HP 10 SONG OF LAUGHTER, *Lauraine Snelling**
__HP 13 PASSAGE OF THE HEART, *Kjersti Hoff Baez*
__HP 14 A MATTER OF CHOICE, *Susannah Hayden*
__HP 18 LLAMA LADY, *VeraLee Wiggins**
__HP 19 ESCORT HOMEWARD, *Eileen M. Berger**
__HP 21 GENTLE PERSUASION, *Veda Boyd Jones*
__HP 22 INDY GIRL, *Brenda Bancroft*
__HP 25 REBAR, *Mary Carpenter Reid*
__HP 26 MOUNTAIN HOUSE, *Mary Louise Colln*
__HP 29 FROM THE HEART, *Sara Mitchell*
__HP 30 A LOVE MEANT TO BE, *Brenda Bancroft*
__HP 33 SWEET SHELTER, *VeraLee Wiggins*
__HP 34 UNDER A TEXAS SKY, *Veda Boyd Jones*
__HP 37 DRUMS OF SHELOMOH, *Yvonne Lehman*
__HP 38 A PLACE TO CALL HOME, *Eileen M. Berger*
__HP 41 FIELDS OF SWEET CONTENT, *Norma Jean Lutz*
__HP 42 SEARCH FOR TOMORROW, *Mary Hawkins*
__HP 45 DESIGN FOR LOVE, *Janet Gortsema*
__HP 46 THE GOVERNOR'S DAUGHTER, *Veda Boyd Jones*
__HP 49 YESTERDAY'S TOMORROWS, *Linda Herring*
__HP 50 DANCE IN THE DISTANCE, *Kjersti Hoff Baez*
__HP 53 MIDNIGHT MUSIC, *Janelle Burnham*
__HP 54 HOME TO HER HEART, *Lena Nelson Dooley*
__HP 57 LOVE'S SILKEN MELODY, *Norma Jean Lutz*
__HP 58 FREE TO LOVE, *Doris English*
__HP 61 PICTURE PERFECT, *Susan Kirby*
__HP 62 A REAL AND PRECIOUS THING, *Brenda Bancroft*
__HP 65 ANGEL FACE, *Frances Carfi Matranga*
__HP 66 AUTUMN LOVE, *Ann Bell*
__HP 69 BETWEEN LOVE AND LOYALTY, *Susannah Hayden*

*Temporarily out of stock.

(If ordering from this page, please remember to include it with the order form.)